Me and Caleb

by Franklyn E. Meyer

SCHOLASTIC BOOK SERVICES

New York Toronto London Auckland Sydney Tokyo

ISBN 0-590-32269-9

Copyright © 1982 by Franklyn E. Meyer. All rights reserved. Published by Scholastic Book Services, a division of Scholastic Inc.

12 11 10 9 8 7 6 5 4 3 2 1   4   2 3 4 5 6 7/8

Me and Caleb

I don't know where you live, but me and Caleb live in Harleyville, Missouri. Caleb is my little brother, and he always does smart-alecky things to get me in trouble. Harleyville isn't too big, when you compare it to Joplin or Kansas City, but it's lots bigger and more modern than Malta Bend or Humus or any of the other towns in Ogano County, except Queenston, which is the county seat and is where the jail is. Papa is always reminding me and Caleb about the jail so that we'll be good. Me and Caleb have never been out of Missouri, but when we grow up and start to work, we'll probably travel clear around the world. Right now, Harleyville is just about our size. There's always a lot to do, and we have fun just trying to keep out of trouble.

Take for instance the time we got Petunia. That was last spring. It was one of those nights that are too hot for early spring, when the sky clouds up just before dark, all ready to storm for sure, and then just sits up there and doesn't rain a drop.

It was so hot we just lay in our beds and worked at falling asleep. Somehow that night I got to thinking about dogs. The thing is, my mother had a little dachshund called Weenie, a good little dog and man's best friend and all that, but not the kind of dog that does anything for a kid's standing. Now Dink Fowler had a big meat grinder of a bulldog called Rupert that he was always talking up as a fighter, and I got to thinking about them and pretty soon I was in the middle of a dream and Rupert was going to eat Weenie up and I was trying to get at them and couldn't and —

"They're in here again," said Caleb, and I woke up.

"They get in here every night," continued Caleb.

I turned over and tried to go back to sleep.

"You'd think somebody'd come up here in daylight and spray Flit around the room and try to kill some of them," mused Caleb.

"Well, they're not over here, so how's about shutting up and letting me get some sleep?"

"It isn't the biting," continued Caleb, like he was talking to himself and hadn't heard me. "That's the least part of it, the biting. It's that darn buzzing they always make before

2

they do it. They just do that buzzing in your ears like that so you can't get to sleep and forget about them."

"Put the pillow over your head," I suggested.

I waited a minute or two, while the sheets rustled in the bed next to mine. Then Caleb's voice came through again, muffled and far away.

"Camn't breave!" he seemed to be saying.

"Yeah," I said, and started thinking about dogs again. I couldn't help but hear the rapid in-breathing and out-breathing from Caleb's side of the bedroom. Finally it settled down to normal again. I was just drifting off again when the breathing started up faster. I listened.

"Smmm-smmm-smmm," said Caleb.

He did this for four or five minutes and then sat up in his bed and did it some more.

"Smell it?" he said at last. I let him talk. "Hey, Bud! What's in here that stinks?"

I sniffed. "Smm-smm-smm."

Caleb was right; something smelled bad in the air in our room.

"You change socks this week?" asked Caleb.

"Sure I did," I answered. "It's not coming from over here, anyway; it's coming from all over."

We got up and began sniffing around our

room. I smelled the closet, even the shoes, and it wasn't that. It was a different smell. Caleb checked under the beds and didn't find anything there either.

"Hey!" I said. "Come here, Caleb." He joined me at the window, which overlooked the porch on our side yard. "Smell?" I asked him.

"Smmm-smmm-smmm? Yeah! It's from somewhere down there. Come on. Let's go see what it is! Come on, Bud!"

From long practice we had no trouble making our way quietly across the porch roof and down to the ground, by way of my oak tree. It was *my* oak tree because it had my tree house in it.

When we got down on the ground, we sniffed around for a while but couldn't get the scent again.

"I wonder what it was," said Caleb, longingly.

"I don't know," I answered. "Well, we better get back upstairs. It's after eleven."

"Wait! Hey, Bud! Smmm-smmm-smmm! I got it again. I smell it," said Caleb. As he followed the trail, he held his arms out to the sides like he thought he was an airplane or something. He banked and headed toward the bushes around at the back of our house, and I followed.

After a few circles and clover leaves, Caleb (like me, still in his underpants) went down on a point, right at the entrance to the crawl space that extended under our house. The floors of our house stood about three feet above the level of the ground. At the back, just under the kitchen window, the bricks had been laid in an arch so plumbers and little children could find a hide-out or a repair job, whichever it was they wanted.

"It's in there," said Caleb, dramatically. "That's where the smell comes from. Whatever it is that stinks is under our house."

"Good dog," I said. "Now go under there and see what it is, so I can get back to sleep."

Caleb began a slow duck-waddle into the blackness of that crawl space. His bare feet made no sound on the soft dust. I waited and watched. Above me a cloud with silver edges drifted over a small patch of stars; I heard a cow lowing from a farm pasture somewhere just outside of town. Then I heard the worst noise I ever heard.

It was like a low, hoarse whinny from a sick horse, one with a hairball in his throat, or whatever it is they get in their throats. It could have been a laugh or a cry of pain or I don't know what all, but it came rolling out of that pitch black like something insane, something out of another world.

Caleb came out of the crawl space too. He was duck-waddling at approximately 25 m.p.h., and I don't mean maybe, when he passed me, and he didn't straighten up until he was forty or fifty feet away from the house. He said, "Holy Mackerel!" as he went by. I went over and joined him pretty quick myself.

"Who whinnied?" he asked, with great sincerity, looking at me like maybe I should know.

"Not me!" I said. "Whatever it was, that noise came from under the house,"

"You figured that all out by yourself, did you? Why'd you think I came out from under there, because I was lonesome?"

"Well, what was it?" I asked.

"I didn't stop to find out," said Caleb, bitterly. "Why, I couldn't see *anything* under there, not a thing. And just as I got up under the living room, WHEHEEHEEHEE! Right there in front of me. I almost fainted. I stood up and almost put my head through the hall floor. I think I was unconscious. I got away from that noise, though."

"Yeah, I noticed," I said.

"Bud, what do you think it is? What could it be?" Caleb pleaded.

For some reason I wasn't scared. Maybe I wasn't completely awake yet, or maybe I just wanted to show Caleb up for a change. I was curious, yes; but not scared.

"Let's find out," I heard myself saying. "Slip into the kitchen and grab the flashlight out of the drawer. I'll go and see."

Caleb looked at me for a second.

"You're nuttier than a hickory grove," he said, and then he went for the flashlight.

After he brought it, I worked my way just inside the brick wall. I turned on the flashlight and began to shine the beam around. I couldn't see much of anything except dust and a few rocks and a section of rusty pipe from a repair job some time ago.

"WHEHEEHEEHEEHEEHEEHEE!"

When it started, I braced myself, like I had when I shot Gramps' twelve-gauge last Thanksgiving. The beam of the flashlight only shook for a minute. It seemed to me that the noise came from behind the chimney, which extended down into the crawl space. I worked myself over toward it on my elbows and knees. Outside I could still hear Caleb's nervous whisper.

"Hey, Bud? You all right? Hey, Bud? You all right, Bud?"

Soon as I got around the corner of the chimney, I began to feel a lot better, for I found myself looking at the tan flanks of some

7

animal, presumably a dog. The dog was breathing hard, and on each breath it looked like the rib bones would punch out through the skin. Before I even got to where I could see its face, I detected movement in the shadows around its belly, and, changing the position of the flashlight (I had been holding it with my mouth), I saw a pup with a face weezened up like a caterpillar. He was attempting to nurse, but there was nothing there for him. Beside the caterpillar, I noticed the swollen and decomposing bodies of two other pups. This explained the smell. Then I scooted closer and looked into the eyes and face of that big dog, and somehow I knew that I was going to call her Petunia.

She was a great big dog. She was about the size of a Great Dane with her body stretched out more like a dachshund. Somehow she had gotten the hairy, protruding eyebrows of an Airedale, and the sagging muzzle and ears of a hound. Petunia had short brown hair, and her tail might have been transplanted from a collie.

"Hello, girl," was all I could think of to say. She lifted her head up and looked over her flanks, and over her live pup, and over her dead pups, and at me, who she couldn't even see because of the glaring flashlight. And that ridiculous tail thumped once in the dust, and then she laid her head back down. I guess she just figured the game was up.

She didn't even make that terrible noise when I picked up her pup and held it up next to me and wondered what to do when it nuzzled against me.

I guess I cried under there, under the house, that spring evening. It seemed so sad for those little puppies to be dead before they even had a chance at the world. I heard Caleb continuing to ask me if I was all right, but I was too interested in Petunia and her puppy to answer him. That was a mistake. I should have answered Caleb.

Later he told everyone that he thought something had "got" me when I went around the corner of the chimney and he couldn't see me anymore. I guess, considering the way that Caleb's mind works, this is logical; but I never quite understood it.

He burst into the kitchen, screaming: "It's got Bud! It's got him under the house! Help! Quick! It's got Bud!"

With these soothing words on his lips, he dashed upstairs and into the placid darkness of my parents' room, with Weenie behind him, yapping like crazy. Weenie slept in the kitchen.

"It's got Bud, under the house!" Caleb

shouted, shaking Papa's sore shoulder, like he was trying to pluck a ripe gourd off of a tough vine. Papa was always slow to wake up, except in times of emergency, and (according to Mama), he just sat up in bed and tried to work his arm back into joint.

"What is it, Caleb? What's the matter?" Mama said.

"It's got Bud, and it whinnies. Hurry fast, and bring the first-aid kit."

"Oh, it's all right," said Papa, slowly beginning to come to. "I'll get it back in place in a minute. I don't need any first-aid kit."

"It's not for you, Orville, it's for Bud," Mama explained.

"Why, Bud's arms are as sturdy as timber. Why in heaven's name does he need first-aid?"

"Because it's got him," said Mama emphatically. "That's what Caleb has been telling us. It's got Bud under the house, and it whinnies."

That kind of statement from Mama must have spelled "emergency" to Papa, because he woke up all at once and jumped out of bed like the hot water bottle was leaking.

"It does what?" Papa inquired. "What does it do?"

"It whinnies, and smells terrible," Caleb informed him. Papa thought this over for only a second or two. "Call the police," he ordered

Mama. "And Caleb, you go get your baseball bat."

The noise that Caleb had made coming upstairs must have waked Callie — that's my sister. Anyway, she arrived just in time to get in on the last bit of the conversation. In her sleepy and confused condition, she immediately assumed that Papa and Caleb were arming themselves to come down to her room and bat her parrot to death, something that Papa had been threatening to do for four years.

"Don't do it! Please don't do it!" she pleaded. "He only talked tonight because I had the light on and left the hood off of his cage. It's not his fault! It's mine. Beat me with your baseball bats. Go ahead and hit me, not that poor bird who never did anything to anybody, except talk once in a while when you wanted to go to sleep."

Stopping in the doorway, Papa looked at Mama.

"I never said Bud couldn't talk at night. What is this, anyway? I don't want to hit her with a bat. I just want to get Bud out from under the house and away from that thing that whinnies and stinks."

"It sure can whinny," added Caleb.

"It does not!" said Callie. "It cheeps and it caws; but it doesn't whinny!"

"I was there, I ought to know," said Caleb.

"Oh, yeah?" replied Callie. "Well, it lives in my room and I feed it and clean up after it and I should know what kind of noises it makes better than you do!"

"Good night!" yelled Papa. "What kind of nut hatch is this, anyway? Callie keeps it in her room and it's got Bud under the house, and it smells bad and it whinnies, and I don't know what all else. Why can't you get things organized around here?" he flung at Mama. Then he stalked down the stairs to get me out from under the house.

When the police came, there was nobody to shoot, arrest, or apprehend. The only suspicious character around was Papa, who stood muttering to himself over by the honesuckle vine, next to the garage. When things get too much for him in our family, Papa likes to act like he's been driven clear round the bend. I guess it was lucky the police knew him.

I carried Petunia into the kitchen, and Mama fixed some warm milk and some medicine for the poison that someone had fed her. She took it and didn't throw it up, as everybody thought she would. But Small Fry, the pup, couldn't quite make it on the beginning he got. The next day we made a little grave for him down in one corner of our lot. And me and Caleb kept the lawn watered around the grave so it looked real nice even through the summer and fall.

 **2**

Our town is situated on the edge of the Ozark Mountains, which, as I understand it, is an old, beat-up range that was all torn down by the glaciers a long time ago. Anyway, they're too small to get any real national attention, and they just sit there like little blisters left over from all that ice rubbing across the ground. Most of the farming around here is done in the flat land that spreads out from these mountains northward.

Since we're the biggest city in our end of the county, Harleyville is kind of a shopping center for the farmers.

In the hills there is lots of second growth timberland that will some day be valuable for railroad ties. Right now this woodland makes fine cover for deer, coon, possum, rabbit, skunk, quail, squirrel, some turkey and otter, black snakes, copperheads, and cottonmouth water moccasins. All through the hills there

14

are small rivers and creeks full of catfish, bluegill, perch, carp, buffalo, and bass. Each spring, and sometimes in the fall, these waterways get up out of their banks and go spewing down into the Gingham River, about five miles south of here.

The summers are miserably hot — dust and chiggers and whole months without rain. We eat good in the summer, though. Lots of new, yellow ears of field corn, fat red tomatoes, thick-hided, black-seeded watermelons that come apart in your mouth like cold candy; fried chicken every Sunday with milk gravy and mashed new potatoes and maybe a strawberry pie with a couple of feet of whipped cream on top to finish off with. Everybody moves outside in the summer, especially at night. Grown-ups get together to swat mosquitoes and pitch horseshoes or play croquet. The kids swat mosquitoes too, and play kick-the-can under a street light somewhere, or Monopoly on a screened back porch, if we can find one. On hot afternoons (and that's just about the only kind there is, in summer) we sometimes go out to one of the creeks in our neighborhood for a swim, riding out the five miles on our bikes, eating dust all the way, and gulping a gallon of iced tea when we finally get home. During the day we try to avoid trouble, or, if worst comes to worst, we mow lawns in the neighborhood to get enough money to go to the movie in the afternoon.

In winter it never really gets very cold, according to the thermometer, but it's damp and cloudy almost all the time, with wet snows to clog things up now and then. Our little town is mostly gray and white and black in the winter, drab and boring. But it makes the lighted windows at night look a lot more cozy, especially when there's a homemade wreath hanging on the front door and it's the house where you were born and you know it's the place where you belong.

Springs and falls around here are something to behold. Every spring the dogwood bursts out all through the woods, and a little later the wild plum does too. The mud settles out of the rivers and streams, and the mayflies float on the green water. Day and night the air smells like wild honey and you want to get out there in all the new, green things and jump like a rabbit. At least I do. We have a lot of picnics then.

Almost every Easter we go down to Gramps' farm. Me and Caleb and Callie are too old for all that Easter Rabbit stuff, so we go down to the farm and have a big dinner instead. Last Easter we went hand-fishing too.

The day was a real peach, even for April. The sky seemed like it hadn't even heard there was such a thing as clouds, and there was just a touch of wind that you could only notice when you stood in the shade for a while. All the brown fields were green now, and pushing upward — a big improvement over the wet, brown soil that we'd looked at all winter. The garden had already been planted, and if you looked close, you could just begin to see the tiny radish leaves popping out of the ground. The potato rows were sectioned off into mounds that looked like they might erupt at any minute.

The robins had come back early, and just about everywhere you looked you'd see one of them making off with a chicken feather or a twig to be a part of their new nests. Or else they'd be lined up like a row of bobbing machines, out by the feeding trays in the chicken yard, gulping down that laying mash like they were Rhode Island Reds.

The hens were leading around raggedy squads of adolescent chicks, who were right in the middle of changing from fuzz to feathers and looked like they had mange. There were new March pigs grunting around down in the hog lot, and there was one new calf frisking in the barn lot, with two more expected at any time.

Mama and Callie had gone right in to help Grandma with the big noontime meal that we always ate when we were at the farm. Gramps said that country folks always had their big meal at noon, " 'cause they need their strength for a full afternoon of work." And whether it's Sunday or Christmas or even your birthday, when you're a farmer there's always a full afternoon of work to do.

When we first got there, Gramps showed me and Caleb and Papa all around the farm, like he always did, so that we'd be sure to notice the improvements since we'd been there last. After that, he and Papa went back up on the front porch and smoked and talked.

"What'll we do?" asked Caleb.

"We could go down in the woods and climb trees," I offered.

"Aw-w, we always climb trees. Hey, I got it! Let's go fishing, Bud! It's warm enough, and we might do some good."

Gramps had a creek running through one corner of his farm, and me and Caleb had always had pretty good luck there.

"Yeah!" I agreed. "Let's get the poles."

"And worms. We'll need lots of worms."

We dug two or three dozen down at the lower end of the garden, the part which hadn't been planted yet. The way me and Caleb dug for worms, you wouldn't have to plow that ground to use it, and I think that's just why Gramps had sent us down there. Then we got Papa to get the poles down from the rafters in the garage.

"It's only an hour or so until dinner," he cautioned, "and I don't want to have to come looking for you two."

"No, sir," I said.

"By the way," said Gramps, as we got ready to go, "there's a lot of eels in that creek, and you may run into some of them. There's not a man in Ogano County who can hold onto an eel unless he knows how to."

"Who wants to?" said Caleb. I agreed.

"You would, if you'd ever tasted one. You pickle them in vinegar and sugar. And I tell you, they're fine!"

Caleb looked at me, and we both knew right then that we weren't eating any eels, pickled, scalped, or dipped in chocolate sauce.

"The only way you can handle them," Gramps continued, "is to loop your middle finger over them and leave your other fingers underneath. Then when you squeeze, it puts a bend in the eel so he can't slide out of your hand. Get it?"

I got it. So did Caleb.

"Well, if you catch any eels, you bring them home, understand?" ordered Gramps.

"Yeah," said Caleb.

"Sure, Gramps," I said.

We took off through the barn lot and down the hill, me carrying the poles and Caleb carrying the worms and tackle box.

"If I even *see* an eel," Caleb commented, "I'm going to throw my pole in the creek and come home." Caleb was walking behind me, because he didn't like to look out for snakes, and I didn't mind.

Spring is one of the worst times of the year for snakebite in our part of the country. On warm days in April and May, the copperheads and moccasins come out of their rocky holes and lie where the sun can hit them. Copperheads are the worst. Even in the middle of summer they don't try to get away from you. They just lie there and wait, looking exactly like the rocks and grass around them. And Lord help the feller who plants a size ten in their vicinity, because he's going to get hit! I'd heard all the stories about snakes, but hadn't ever gotten mixed up with one close up. Maybe that's why I was confident.

When we got to the bottom of the hill, we made our way carefully through a wide meadow where the heavy bluegrass was beginning to grow up through the dead stalks from last year. Gramps' cows spend most of their time in that meadow, because the grass is so rich. In the middle of it was the creek. Just as we caught sight of it, a great big bass flopped over, out in the middle, and me and Caleb ran the rest of the way.

It took us a few minutes to convince the worms onto our hooks and get our lines unrolled from the poles and rigged. We held on to our poles, waiting for the corks to start bobbing.

When they didn't, we pushed the ends of the poles into the soft mud on the creek bank and waited some more. Nothing happened.

After a while Caleb looked over at me.

"What's the matter with those dumb fish anyhow?" he asked me.

"Maybe they're not hungry," I suggested.

"Maybe they're not, but I sure am. You think it's about time for dinner?" he asked.

"I guess so," I answered. "We might as well go on back. Fish just aren't hungry."

We wound up our lines and went back to ths house, disappointed with our luck but pleased by the smell we caught when we got near the kitchen.

Grandma had done up two or three fryers, and there were peas and milk gravy and mashed potatoes and biscuits and everything else, to go with the fried chicken. Mama brought out a great big devil's food cake for dessert, with all the extra icing we wanted to put on top of it, and me and Caleb ate so much we almost died.

"Couldn't do any good, huh?" asked Gramps, while the women cleared off the table. We were so stuffed we could just sit there like a couple of Easter eggs, staring at one another.

"Nope," I said, with effort.

"The fish weren't hungry, Gramps," Caleb added.

"You ought to stay around until evening," Gramps went on. "I'd show you some real fishing." Gramps was working away on his mouth with a toothpick, and it was kind of hard to understand him. "None of those baby bream and perch either. Real fish!"

"Where would you get those fish to show us?" Caleb wanted to know.

Gramps just laughed. Then he turned to Papa.

"Any chance of you staying a little late tonight, Orville? I'd enjoy taking those boys hand-fishing. They're old enough now, and it's been a good year for it — some big buffalo and cats lately. They're getting them over at the river."

Papa had been raised in St. Louis, so he didn't know any more about hand-fishing than me and Caleb did.

"*What* kind of fishing?" Papa asked.

"With your hands, at night," Gramps answered. "You get a boat and a lantern and a gunny sack. Then you find a hole about three or four feet deep and work your way along the bank, feeling in among the roots and logs until you find a fish. They won't move, either. You just grab them and throw them in the sack."

"You mean you can really catch fish that way?" asked Papa.

"Why, sure!" said Gramps. "It's one of the best ways I know of."

"Can we, Papa?" asked Caleb.

"Please, Papa?" I added.

Papa looked into the kitchen where Mama was drying dishes. Mama just shrugged her shoulders.

"Well, I guess so," said Papa.

So that night, just about dark, me and Caleb and Gramps took the pick-up truck and drove about a mile and a half, over to the river. The Gingham gets wide right where Gramps kept his rowboat, and after fishing in that silly little creek at the farm, that river looked like an ocean or something.

In a few minutes we were out on that black water, with Gramps rowing us to some hand-fishing place that he knew about.

"Now, don't forget what I told you about an eel. Middle finger over his back, and the rest of your fingers under him. I'm sure hungry for a good mess of pickled eels," Gramps reminded us when we got to the place.

It was fully dark by then, and the frogs and early tree toads were whooping it up from the willow trees that lined the shore.

"This is the spot, all right," said Gramps, in a low tone, poking his oar down to the bottom to make sure it was the right depth. "Now skinny out of your clothes and over the side."

"What?" said Caleb.

"Take off your clothes. You've got to wade in the water up to your neck if you're going to hand-fish," explained Gramps. I don't think Caleb had realized this before.

"We've got to do what?" demanded Caleb.

"Get into the water," said Gramps. "It's only about three feet deep here."

"In the water?" asked Caleb.

"Well, sure! How do you expect to grab those fish if you aren't in the water?" inquired Gramps, patiently.

"I don't," said Caleb. "The only thing I'm going to grab is that oar, in case I see something moving out on the water."

"Oh, sassafras," said Gramps. "Maybe you're too little to go hand-fishing after all."

That did it. I skinned out of my clothes and stood there in the front of the boat for a moment, shivering in the damp river air.

"I'll do it," I said, sounding braver than I felt.

"That a boy!" encouraged Gramps.

"Sucker!" Caleb chided.

The water was surprisingly warm. I lowered myself down into its blackness, holding firmly to the side of the boat. I'll admit that I was going strictly on nerve; I'd rather have done *anything* than climb into that river, but I couldn't chicken out in front of Gramps. And anyhow, I was showing Caleb up!

Slowly as I could, I let myself down until the water stood right around my waist. I kept pointing down, with my big toe, to find the bottom. Finally I found it.

"What the dickens!" said Gramps. "Why're you sitting on my lap? I thought you weren't afraid to get in the water."

"What's that stuff on the bottom?"

"What stuff?"

"That slimy stuff. I tried to stand up on it and sank clear up to my ankles. That stuff's terrible."

"What did I tell you?" Caleb smirked.

"It's just mud on the river bottom," said Gramps. He said it like that made it all right, but it didn't.

"Cripes," I complained, "it hasn't got a bottom."

"Sure it has," said Gramps. "It's only a foot and a half deep at the most. Just plain old mud."

I went back in. My toes felt their way carefully through about a foot of the junk on the bottom before I hit solid ground. I stood there a minute and tried to get used to it. The moon had come up now, and it made a silver coating on the water before me, and I felt like a head and shoulders floating around on top of the water with no lower part attached. All of a sudden I remembered those big snapping turtles I'd seen laying out on logs sunning themselves the last time we'd come out to the river.

"Any turtles around here?" I asked Gramps.

"If there are, they'll get out of your way fast enough," Gramps assured me.

"Well, they better, or I will. What do I do next?"

"Work your way over to that bank over there while I light the lantern. When you get there, feel around the roots of that big willow tree growing at the edge of the water. When you feel a fish, grab him through the gills and haul him out here. We'll put him in the sack. And don't forget about how to catch eels!"

I wouldn't know an eel from an alligator, I thought, but I made my way up to the bank that he'd pointed to. It was even scarier away from the boat. You never knew what to expect when you put your foot down in that slime, and the depth of the water changed every few yards.

When I got near the bank, I felt right under those tree roots, just like Gramps had told me to do. Way back in one corner of the hollow, beneath the tree, my hand hit something cold and soft, different from anything else I had touched in the water. I yanked my hand back.

"Hey!" I yelled. "I felt something!"

"Well, of course you did," Gramps hollered back. "What do you think we're doing out here, playing hide-and-seek?"

I knew we weren't playing hide-and-seek, so I went back to that willow and felt in the hole again. Whatever it was, it was still there. Slowly, and very softly, I felt along the thing. I felt a fin. It was bigger than anything I had ever caught on a hook and line. Suddenly I forgot about the goo underfoot and the turtles and everything else. I just wanted that fish. I had to have it.

I felt him again, and figured that he was facing out, toward the river where I was standing. Carefully, I found the gill slit and poked my thumb up into it, fast and hard, the way Gramps had said. And I held on.

At first it felt like the end of my arm was going to get pulled off. I wrestled that fish out of the hole and lost my balance, ducking completely under the water. But I held on. Finally that fish got tired of fighting, and I pulled him out.

"I've got him!" I shouted. "I've got him!"

"What is it, an eel?" yelled Gramps.

"It feels like a bull," I said, making my way toward the light of the lantern.

When I got him to the boat, Gramps held the light down to see what I'd caught.

"Good one, Bud. It's a carp. Nice size, too," Gramps said. Caleb just stared at my fish with his mouth open.

"Did you really catch that thing with your hands?" he asked.

"Sure," I said proudly. Caleb began to undress.

"How's the water, Bud?" he asked me.

"Fine," I said. My carp was flopping around in the sack at the bottom of the boat.

The first thing you know, Caleb had grabbed himself a buffalo just a little bit smaller than my carp.

"This is really great!" Caleb said to me as we started back for another try.

"You betcha!" I sung out.

I tried underneath an old log that slanted down into the water from the bank. Again I felt a fish, but this time I must have scared him or something, because he flopped his tail and was gone.

"I get the next one!" insisted Caleb.

The next spot turned out to be a kind of cave at the bottom of a small limestone cliff.

"That's a dandy," whispered Caleb, working his way over to the opening in the rock. The water got a little deeper there, and Caleb had to stand on his tiptoes and point his chin up in the air to keep above water.

"Too deep?" I asked him hopefully. "You want me to get this one?"

"Unn . . . nope!" said Caleb. He sounded funny, talking in that position. I watched as he worked his way right up next to the cave.

"I'm reachin' in now." he whispered. "Sides are all smooth." His head was inside the cave now. I couldn't see him, but I could hear him. His voice echoed in there. "Can't seem to find the end of it," he went on. "Whoa!"

"What's the matter?" I asked.

"Just brushed by something. Felt like another buffalo. A bigger one."

"Well, get it!" I urged.

"I'm trying," he said. "Holy Crow, Bud, it's round!"

"What?"

"This thing is round, not flat like a fish."

"Good-bye, Caleb," I said.

"Wait a minute, Bud. It's big, too, bigger than my arm."

"Well, you stand there and measure it. I'm going back to the boat," I told him.

"Hold on. I think it's an eel!"

"How do you know?" I asked.

"I don't know. But it feels the way Gramps says they feel. Long and slick."

"Well, if you're not afraid, put your middle finger over him and squeeze, so he can't get away."

"All right," said Caleb. "Gramps won't think I'm a sissy when I bring him an eel, will he, Bud?"

"I don't guess he will," I answered, with an odd feeling in my stomach.

"Well, here goes!" said Caleb. I heard the water in that little cave begin thrashing around, like when you give a cat a bath.

"I've got him!" shouted Caleb. "Man, he's big. He's wrapping all around my arm."

"Well, don't lose him, for Pete's sake. Drag him back to the boat."

"I can't pull him out of this cave, Bud, he's pulling too hard."

"Try," I said. Slowly Caleb worked his way out of the cave and over to where Gramps was sitting in the boat. I was right behind him. Gramps was holding up the lantern and peering at us.

"What's all the commotion?" he wanted to know. "You boys have another one already?"

"I got an eel for you, Gramps!" Caleb said proudly.

"Hot darn!" said Gramps. "There's nothing like a good mess of pickled eel."

By then we were up to the boat, and Gramps held the sack open for Caleb. With the other hand he held the lantern over our heads.

"Go ahead, throw him in, Caleb!" ordered Gramps. "And don't let go until he's inside the sack."

Caleb pulled and grunted until he had his arm just under the water.

"He's all twined around my arm," he explained. "He's not going to let go."

Slowly Caleb's arm came up out of the water.

Twined around it, from his hand all the way to his shoulder, was the biggest cottonmouthed water moccasin I had ever seen in my life, even in the zoo at Joplin. Its head still dangled off in the water somewhere.

Caleb, of course, wouldn't know a water moccasin from a ukulele. But me and Gramps knew. We both just froze, staring at all that snake.

"Let go there, you big old eel, you," laughed Caleb, shaking his arm as he held it over the sack. "Go ahead and get him, Gramps!"

"NO!" hollered Gramps. "And don't shake him anymore!"

"Huh?" said Caleb. He was confused by Gramps' different-sounding voice. "Why can't I shake him off in the bag, Gramps? Does that make them taste bad, or something?"

"Just don't do it," commanded Gramps, getting his voice back under control. "Just stand still. You hear me? Don't move!"

"Why, Gramps?" said Caleb. "You mean to say you're afraid of a little old eel? And you the one that likes to eat them so much!"

"It's a —" I started to say, but Gramps cut me off.

"Shut up, Bud," he warned. By the lantern light I could see that sweat had popped out all over his face.

"Boo, Gramps!" laughed Caleb, poking the snake up at him.

"Cut that out!" roared Gramps.

"You just put your middle finger over them and your other fingers under them and squeeze," teased Caleb.

"Caleb . . . uh . . . let it go, real easy, in the water. Let that eel go," Gramps persuaded. "He's too little to keep. It's uh . . . against the law to keep them if they're that small."

"Too little?" argued Caleb, angrily. "Why, if he'd been any bigger, he'd have put me in a sack!"

"Well, just let go of him, Caleb."

"No, I'm not going to let him go," insisted Caleb. "I'll put him in that sack myself, if you're too scared to."

And with that, he threw his leg over the side of the boat and climbed right in, snake and all.

The sudden weight on the boat's side and Gramps' decision to visit the other end of the boat at the same time brought about the results you might expect. The next thing I knew, Gramps was splashing around in the water next to me, the lantern hissed and went out, and Caleb was yelling about his eel. After a while, Gramps managed to get the boat right side up, with most of the water out of it, and he and I climbed in. Caleb was still standing in the waist-deep water.

"Quick, get him in the boat!" hollered Gramps.

"Caleb," I said, helping him aboard, "Caleb, are you all right?"

"Sure," he said, mad as can be, "but you two nitwits let my big eel get away."

When we'd made sure that Caleb wasn't snake-bitten anywhere, Gramps kind of wilted over the middle seat of the boat, and I got out and pulled the boat back to where we had left the truck. We'd lost all our fish — and our taste for fishing too.

We told Caleb what it was all about on the way back, and I thought he was going right up through the roof of the truck. We never did tell Mama or Papa about Caleb's "eel" though. All I have to do now, to get a rise out of Gramps, is to ask to go hand-fishing, whenever we're at the farm.

He just looks at me and kind of smiles.

 **3**

I turned twelve years old in June, right after school let out. It was nice to be two years older than Caleb again, but the best thing about it was that I got to keep Petunia. At first Papa had said she could just stay around until she recovered from the poison, but he finally gave in after I worked on him awhile. Mama was harder to convince.

It wasn't that Mama didn't like dogs; Weenie, our dachshund, was more hers than anyone else's. But it would mean extra work for her.

"I can just see what my living room carpet will look like," she said. "All that hair. Why, Weenie alone must shed a couple of bales of it every summer. And that big pot-hound will be ten times worse."

Also, she must have figured that Weenie would be unhappy about the new arrangement, but after the dog fight she agreed with Papa and said I could keep Petunia.

The dog fight happened the day after Papa and I had built the new box for Petunia, out of some pine boards we found in the basement.

We live in an old white frame house on Rainwater Street, right at the edge of town, and there was plenty of room for Petunia to run around without even going out of our yard.

It was a hot Wednesday morning with a lot of big clouds that were too white, as if they might be planning to get together and rain before noon.

I meandered outside after breakfast and tried to think of something interesting to do. The new house they were building next door was almost finished, and they kept it locked, so I couldn't go over there and mess around. And swimming was out because it would probably rain before we could get to the creek.

I almost fell asleep, standing there in our driveway, trying to think up things to do. And then I saw Dink Fowler's red head coming up Rainwater Street. I just stood there with my hands in my pockets while he walked up to me.

"What's the matter, Bud, toothache?" he asked, after he'd stood peering at me awhile.

"Nah. Just haven't got anything to do."

"Me neither," said Dink. "What about that old cat of your Aunt Emma's? We haven't done anything to him for a long time."

"She took him with her when she went on vacation."

"Oh," said Dink. "Where's Caleb?"

"I don't know. Somewhere."

"I knew he was somewhere. Why don't we get our bikes and ride down to Hoofer's?"

"I'm broke."

"Me too. Couldn't we get some money off of Caleb?"

"He yells too loud. And anyway, he hasn't got any money either."

"Well then, how about fighting the dogs? You been yellowing out on that all summer."

Dink Fowler had the only English bulldog in Harleyville, and although the dog was getting old, just looking at that big slobbering jaw and those beady little eyes was enough to make all the dogs around town remember appointments elsewhere. So Dink had kind of a reputation, locally, because everybody agreed that his dog could lick anybody else's dog. This had been going on for about two years, and Dink's dog, Rupert, still hadn't had to defend his title. Just to look at Rupert was enough to make a person, or a dog, look around for the nearest climbable tree.

"Aw, you know Rupert can lick Weenie," I said bitterly.

"Lick him?" Dink laughed. "Why my Rupert could eat that little sausage, collar and all!"

"Dachshunds aren't supposed to be for fighting. They're for hunting rabbits in Germany. They're built like that so that they can run right into the rabbit hole with the rabbit."

"Yeah? Well, I'll bet if that Weenie of yours ever came up face to face with a mean, live rabbit, he'd faint. I bet he'd roll over on his back and pray, if he ever saw a rabbit."

"You do, huh?" I said, feeling the mad coming up through my breakfast.

"Yeah, that's what I think," said Dink, who didn't have red hair for nothing. "And I also think that you and him make a good pair, because you're a yellow stink-pot too!"

I may be bigger than Dink by an inch or so, but I never could handle him any better than he could handle me. One time we fought for forty-five minutes before anybody came along and broke us up. I hadn't liked to fight that hard, and I don't think Dink had either. But now there was nothing I could do except go after him; he'd insulted both me and Weenie.

I socked him in the cheek and felt his fist come ramming into my belly. I hoped somebody would come along and stop us before we killed each other.

I'm not sure how much later it was — the buttons of my shirt had popped off, and my nose was bleeding a little, and Dink had a cut on his forehead and a tear in the knee of his pants — when I realized that Caleb was leaning against the wall of the garage, watching us with great interest while he ate on a cold pork chop.

"Keep your right hand up in front of your chin," he advised me, right after Dink had landed one on my button.

"Why don't you beat it?" I said, puffing and panting like a plowed-out mule.

"Yeah!" Dink added. I think we were both happy to have an excuse to stop fighting.

"What're you two fighting about?"

"He said me and Weenie were yellow," I explained, deciding that an explanation might give me a chance to catch my breath.

"Weenie isn't yellow," Caleb said. "Weenie could last five minutes with that big mutt of yours, Dink, a dog five times as heavy, and still walk away when it was over."

"In a pig's eye, he could," said Dink.

Caleb looked up from his pork chop.

"Well, I'll bet my BB gun against your hunting knife that he could."

Dink considered this proposal.

"Put your hunting knife where your mouth is," chided Caleb.

"It's a bet!" said Dink, striding over to where Caleb was leaning against the garage. They shook hands on it, and Dink went to get Rupert.

"You better get out of here before he gets back with that monster of his," I warned.

"Why?" Caleb asked.

"Why do you think? You know Rupert could bite Weenie in half. We can't let those two fight."

"Sure we can. We're going to. Rupert's getting old, and Weenie's real fast when he's mad. Anyhow, my BB gun is broken."

"Well, when Mama wants to know how Weenie got killed, remember, I didn't have anything to do with it."

"Yeah, I'll remember," said Caleb.

Dink came back in a few minutes, leading that live meat grinder on a short length of rope. Caleb had gotten Weenie and was holding him on his lap.

"Supper time, Rupe!" said Dink. It didn't make me feel any better. I knew then that I should have kept on fighting him. It was much better for me to take a few punches than to have Weenie killed or maimed.

"I brought out the alarm clock, so we can see when five minutes is up," said Caleb. "Anytime you're ready," he added.

Dink untied the rope, and Caleb carried Weenie over so that the two dogs were about four feet apart. When they were both free, they stood there and looked at each other. I didn't want to watch.

Rupert was going through his preliminary warm-ups. This started out with a terrible growl that never entirely stopped and came from way down deep in that chest that looked about two feet wide. As he growled, the hair on both sides of his collar began to stand up on end in a kind of lion effect. He began to circle Weenie on legs as stiff as fence posts, all the time working that big jaw back and forth and licking his big, slobbery lips like he actually was going to eat his opponent.

Weenie, on the other hand, looked like the man without a country. The loose skin around his sad little face sagged with dejection, and he seemed to be having a hard time maneuvering his awkward body around as Rupert circled him. His tail curled under his hind legs, and he looked the way he always did just before he got sick.

The two dogs went around in a circle twice, and then Rupert stopped and shifted his growl into second gear. He scratched the ground with his front paws, like a bull getting ready to charge, and the jaws worked faster and faster. This was the signal that it was about to start.

Weenie was looking back and forth between me and Caleb, hoping for some sign of rescue, and seeing none coming, he did a strange thing.

Just as Rupert began pawing the ground, Weenie threw his head back and yelped. It wasn't a howl or a bark. It was a yelp, a yelp that had in it all of the terror and violence and pain which Weenie must have felt. It was like a prayer, like Job must have cried out about the plague and the pestilence. It only lasted a second, but it was very eloquent. After this was taken care of, Weenie shrugged his little shoulders and prepared to do battle.

But the battle didn't come.

We heard the kitchen screen bang shut, and turned, wondering who it was.

Around the corner of the garage came Petunia. She must have heard Weenie's yelp. But it wasn't the same Petunia I had found dying beneath our house. This Petunia walked slowly toward us with the smooth, confident gait of a killer wolf. She didn't look at me, or Caleb or Dink, or even Weenie. Her soft brown eyes were hard now, like shiny marbles that glistened from a fire inside of her some place that burned so hot you knew she moved with only one purpose.

Petunia looked only at Rupert, and Rupert, frozen in surprise, could only look back. His growl had stopped at Petunia's arrival. So had his jaw-moving and ground-pawing. Rupert just looked, as Petunia came on. I think he realized that he had run his bluff to the limit.

Rupert saw the white teeth and wiry hair of an enormous dog that probably had lived for three years completely independent of masters and owners and veterinarians and dog food and kindness and gentle petting — an individual, self-sufficient, capable of fighting and killing anything that got in her way, while wearing a crazy smile on that Airedale muzzle. In other words, Rupert saw the end of the world, looking square at him on that warm summer day.

He just looked, and Petunia continued to advance, head down, ears back, her tail arching up over her like it was her regimental colors.

Rupert swallowed once. Then he looked at Dink. Then he screamed.

It was definitely not a dog noise. Rupert just looked right up at Dink and screamed.

And then he wheeled and lit out for home, throwing gravel four feet into the air as he went.

We watched him as he went down the driveway, not even slowing down to make the turn onto Rainwater Street. Rupert never looked back; self-preservation was beckoning him home.

"Five minutes are up," said Caleb calmly, as though he'd expected it to work out that way. "Weenie can walk. Go get your knife."

"What do you mean, 'Get the knife?' " Dink raged. "Rupert would have eaten Weenie up if that . . . that old leopard of yours hadn't come up and made him get sick."

"Sick my toenails," I said.

"You know," said Caleb, "if you were to get that knife right now and bring it over here, me and Bud just might not tell everybody we know that Rupert got scared and ran home from a fight. We just might not."

Weenie was wiggling around all over the place, now that it was over, and Petunia sat there and watched him with mild curiosity.

That night I lay in bed and examined the knife. It sure was a beauty.

"You didn't have to give it to me," I said to Caleb. I would have done like you told him. I wouldn't have told anybody."

"That's all right," said Caleb. "Didn't want

it in the first place. Just wanted to get it. Anyway, I fixed my BB gun this afternoon. Works fine again."

"That's good," I said, turning off the light. "And thanks again for the knife."

Petunia's tail thumped softly on the floor, right under my bed. And then we all fell asleep.

4

Everything had been too good until August arrived. The ground was just right, in the spring, for early plowing and there had been plenty of sunshine and rain since then. So the corn and alfalfa were coming on real good around Harleyville. The sun began to shine all day, without a sign of a cloud to give you a minute's shade. It was awfully hot; even the healthy green shoots in the fields began to brown at the edges. And the dust stood in the air like smoke.

On those hot afternoons, me and Caleb used to sit up against the side of the garage where there was a little bit of shade to enjoy. We would usually spend our time out there teasing Weenie or throwing sticks for Petunia to fetch. Most of the gang was away with their parents on trips or at YMCA Camp, so we didn't have much to do except get at each other. August was like Sunday, the time just before school started again, and it hung over our heads like a club, making us meaner than a couple of kinky snakes.

Caleb isn't nearly as big as I am, but he's built a lot heavier. He looks a lot like Mama and Callie, while I take after Papa. At least that's what everybody says.

"That big mutt of yours is digging in the rose bushes again," Caleb informed me one afternoon as we sat in the lengthening shadows. Caleb always pretended he didn't like Petunia, but secretly I knew he did; he just acted that way to spite me.

"Tough bounce," I said. Caleb looked at me for a moment.

"Well, don't just sit there like a boob, get her out of those roses!" he ordered.

"You get her out," I sighed. "You don't like her itching her toenails like that, you get her out of there."

"She isn't my dog, remember? You were going to do *everything* for her if Papa let you keep her, remember?"

"Those aren't my roses, either," I reminded him.

"No," argued Caleb, "but they're my mama's. And we don't like that flea-pot of yours scratching up all the roots."

"Who do you think you are anyway, the inner circle of the Garden Club or something?

They're *my* mama's roses too, you know," I told him, "and if she didn't want my dog digging around in there, I believe she'd tell me, instead of sending a message through you."

"You're a real big jerk, you know that?" said Caleb after a pause. "You just love to pick on little kids, don't you?"

"Not all little kids, Caleb. Just the big-mouthed ones."

"I think I'd rather have an idiot for a brother than you," said Caleb.

"No, you wouldn't. I have one, and it's even worse."

We looked at each other hard for a minute. It was always about this time of the afternoon that we got in a fight.

"Well," said Caleb, "we might as well get it over with."

"Yeah," I agreed. "I guess so." But neither of us moved.

It was too hot. The afternoon heat was enough to make you sweat, just sitting there in the shade.

So we just sat there and thought about fighting while we watched the men put down sod in the front yard of the new house next door.

They had built this house in the lot where we used to play marbles, between Fowler's house and ours. And now they were finishing it up.

Three men were carrying rolls of sod from a truck. They'd put down their load and unroll it and then go back to the truck for more. Me and Caleb found it very interesting to watch those three men unroll that sod. They moved slowly but never stopped, back and forth to the truck, carrying sod. They didn't seem to know it was hot.

Earlier in the summer, that house had been a world of fun. Me and Caleb had played soldier in the trenches they dug first. And we stood right behind the carpenters and watched them nail up the framing for the walls. Later, we climbed around in the rafters and played Tarzan and wrote our initials in the concrete that they poured for the basement. And then one day the boss carpenter, who drove a red truck, told me and Caleb to go home and stay home. So we didn't go back anymore, since that was the way they felt. They locked the place up at night now, anyway.

Two carpenters were still working on the kitchen cabinets though. We had seen them through the windows and heard them singing while they worked. Carpenters seem to be a very happy group. Maybe I'll be one.

After we had sat there against the garage

wall and listened to the carpenters singing and watched those three men unroll sod, me and Caleb forgot about fighting.

"When do you think they'll move in?" Caleb mused.

"Soon, I guess," I answered.

"I wonder if our new neighbors will have any kids," said Caleb.

"I don't know," I said. "Once I saw a man with a moustache and a skinny woman, his wife, I guess. I think they are the owners. They came around once to look at the place. I didn't see any kids, though."

Caleb had been messing around with a piece of two-by-four that had somehow gotten out of Papa's lumber pile in the garage. All of a sudden he stood up and heaved that piece of board with all his might at the new house next door.

"Hey, Petunia! Fetch, girl. Fetch it!" he hollered as he threw.

The two-by-four hit on a little porch which stood just outside the side door of the new house. The board slid right in through the door and vanished into the house where those two carpenters were working and singing. Petunia wasn't far behind that two-by-four, either.

Caleb stood there and smiled at me.

"You said to get her out if I didn't like her digging in Mama's roses. Well, I got her out," he said. We both waited and watched the new house for a few seconds.

First the singing stopped and some yelling started. Or else that song had some bad words in it. The men carrying sod stopped and stared at the new house like they wondered why it had hollered at them like that.

In a minute Petunia came loping out of the new house. Between her jaws was a carpenter's level, about two feet long, that I guess she'd mistaken for the board Caleb threw. And her feet were all pink from wet paint.

A carpenter came running out the door right behind her.

Petunia brought the level over to Caleb and dropped it at his feet. She "arfed!" a few times and wagged her tail, waiting for him to throw it again. I think he would have, too, if that carpenter hadn't parted the hedge between the houses and glared at us.

"Hello," said Caleb.

"Gimme that level back," growled the carpenter.

"She thought it was a piece of two-by-four," explained Caleb, "that I threw for her to retrieve."

"So you was the one that threw that beam!"

said the carpenter. He was getting red in the face. "It slid right into the kitchen and knocked over the can of pink paint I was using. Then that big elephant tracked it all over the house, looking for your piece of wood. And he finally took off carrying my level."

"Oh, she's a very smart dog," I bragged. "She won't ever come back until she gets what you throw, or something like it."

"Well, I'm a very smart carpenter," said the man, advancing through the hedge, "and I don't go back until I get my level."

Petunia must have thought that the carpenter was going to do something bad to me and Caleb with that level. Dogs tell everything by tone of voice, you know, and that carpenter's tone of voice must have said "murder."

That carpenter may not have been a very friendly man, but he sure could climb trees, even smooth-barked sycamores, like the one that stood between our house and the new one next door.

"I wish I could climb trees like that," sighed Caleb, with admiration, as we watched that carpenter claw his way up about fifteen feet of smooth trunk to get to the first limb.

The three men in the front yard had

stopped unrolling their sod and just stood in a little group and talked quietly among themselves as they pointed to the carpenter up in the sycamore tree, with Petunia tearing up the ground all around it.

Finally, Mama came outside and made me put Petunia down in the basement, but by that time the carpenter was way up among the very teeny-tiniest branches of the sycamore tree and still climbing fast. It took Mama about ten minutes to convince the carpenter that Petunia couldn't get out of the basement. Then he slowly climbed down the tree, kind of mumbling to himself.

"MY!" said Mama, when the carpenter got down on solid ground again. "Just look at those overalls!"

"You look at them, lady, my neck doesn't bend that way," yelled the carpenter.

"Won't you send them to me and let me sew them up?" said Mama, trying to be nice.

"I won't let you sew them up or me either. Just give me my level and let me go back to the job, will you? Honest to Pete, a working man has a heck of a time just making a living these days."

And he took his level and stomped back through the hedge and into the new house. The other carpenter was waiting for him, with his hand on the knob of the side door so he could close it in a hurry if Petunia should suddenly reappear.

"Where does it hurt, Alfie?" we heard him say.

We explained it all to Mama. Just as we were about to go inside, the upstairs window of the new house flew open and Alfie's head poked out. He said he was going to sue us and have Petunia "put away," but he never did.

After a little while the three men started carrying sod to the lawn again, and me and Caleb went back to leaning up against the wall of the garage.

"You want to fight now?" Caleb asked me.

"Naw," I said. "It's too hot. We'll get at it tomorrow."

"Okay," said Caleb obligingly. He threw his arm around my shoulder, and we went back to watching those men carrying sod.

5

The next morning, right after Papa left for work, a big yellow moving van backed into the driveway of the new house next door. Me and Caleb could hardly wait to get through with breakfast and out to our favorite spot by the side of the garage, where we could watch our new neighbors arrive. It was hot, for so early in the day, but we just leaned back against the garage and didn't pay any attention to the heat. Around the corner, the screen door banged, and in a minute Petunia appeared. At least her head appeared, sticking around the corner from the shade. She seemed to wonder what we were doing and why. Then Weenie's head popped out, about a foot and a half below Petunia's. Weenie was looking up and must have had an interesting view of Petunia's chin. He waited for her to decide where to go.

Petunia yawned and came on around to us,

nosing between me and Caleb so that we could both scratch her, if we decided to.

When Petunia found that we were too hot and lazy to even scratch her ears, she shuffled back onto the driveway, sniffed at the sod men to make sure they weren't carpenters, and ambled off somewhere. Weenie trotted behind, glad to be going anywhere with his idol.

Pretty soon a new green car pulled up and parked out in front of the new house.

"Is that them?" Caleb inquired. "Are they the people who are moving in next door?"

I watched them carefully as they got out of the car. It was the same man with a moustache and the same skinny woman that I'd seen before. But this time they had two children with them.

"Wow!" I said. "Yep, that's them. But just look what's with them!"

That first kid was a boy about Caleb's age but a lot stockier. He had a look about him that said he could take care of himself. His arms hung almost to the ground, and he had a short, pushed-up nose and a bent-back forehead and short hair that couldn't help but remind you of a monkey. But I didn't watch him for long.

Holding on to her mother's hand was about the prettiest girl I had ever seen, and she looked just about my size! She had long, shiny blond hair that hung all the way down to the waist of a starched cotton dress. She didn't look like the boy at all, thank goodness. They walked across the fresh sod and that girl took little dainty steps, not at all like those big horses at our school did.

And this was going to be my next door neighbor! The most beautiful girl that had ever lived in Harleyville (as far as I could remember) was going to live right next to *my* house!

"Great Scott!" I whispered.

"Looks tough, doesn't he?" answered Caleb, who still thought that girls were just a good place to keep hair ribbons.

The mother and father and the two kids all went inside to see how the moving men were doing, and me and Caleb waited, almost holding our breaths, for them to come out again.

"I think I can handle him all right," mused Caleb. "Those heavy ones are always suckers for a stiff punch in the breadbasket."

"Caleb," I warned, "you mustn't pick on that little kid next door. You are much taller than he is, and it would not be a fair fight. Just be nice to him so that we can be their friends."

Caleb gave me a funny look.

"You been out in the sun too long," he said. "I'm gonna have to lick that kid before noon.

If you don't start newcomers off on the right foot, they start taking over on you."

Soon the boy came out of the front door and stood in the front yard, looking around for something to do. He looked something like a baby gorilla that has just been let out of his cage, and I noticed that Caleb was getting a little pale as he watched him.

Finally, that kid's eyes came to rest on a young elm tree that the three men had planted the day before. He loped across the lawn like he thought he was in Africa or somewhere, and his hands did almost touch the ground as he went. When he got over to that baby elm, we could see his smile from clear over where we were sitting. It was a very odd smile.

"Is that kid all right?" asked Caleb uneasily.

Before I could answer, the kid leaned over and grabbed that elm tree just above the ground and yanked the whole blasted thing right out of the ground and up over his head, like it was a feather. And he held it up there, with a great big ball of dirt still clinging to the roots.

"Good night!" whispered Caleb. "Where can I go hide?"

"Lawrence?" A voice from the open front door sounded, and the man with the moustache came out of that house like an exploding firecracker. He grabbed little Lawrence and played a drum solo on his seat that would have put blisters on a catcher's mitt.

"He sure needed that," said Caleb approvingly. Lawrence didn't even whimper, however. When it was over, the man set him down and replaced the elm tree in the hole. Then he tamped the dirt all round it with his feet. Lawrence just smiled and watched. The man with the moustache said some more things to him and pointed to the elm tree as he said them, before going back inside the house.

Soon as he was gone, Lawrence pulled that poor elm tree out of the ground again, like he was plucking a radish, and this time he busted it square in half over his knee, sneering in the direction of the house as he finished the job.

Caleb looked over at me. I never remembered seeing Caleb look like that before. His mouth looked sick, and his eyes didn't have any shine to them at all.

"What'll I do?" he begged me. "Where'll I go?"

"Just sit tight," I cautioned him. "Take it easy."

"Take it easy!" he yelled. "That little monster is gonna come strolling over here in a minute and pinch me in half. I *can't* take it easy, I've got to *do* something!"

"Too late," I said, nodding my head toward the new house.

Lawrence had heard us. After he had finished destroying that elm tree, he looked around and spied us leaning up against the garage wall. For a minute he just stood there and stared at us. He looked like he wasn't sure whether we were supposed to be broken over his knee, like that elm tree, or peeled and eaten, like a banana. He leaned over and picked something up from the ground.

"See you around, Bud," said Caleb, starting around the corner of the garage. But that rock caught him just above the knee of his right leg.

"Throws real good, too, doesn't he?" remarked Caleb, as he limped back to where I still leaned against the garage.

"Pretty fair," I agreed. "Don't worry, Caleb. I'll protect you," I added. "Hey, you!" I yelled at him over the hedge. "COMMERE!"

I said it as tough as I knew how. Lawrence stared at me suspiciously for a second. Then he picked up the old piece of two-by-four that had started all the trouble the day before. He walked up to the hedge, parted it with both hands, and looked at me.

"Well, so long, Bud," said Caleb, disappearing around the corner of the garage. Lawrence stayed by the hedge and waited for me to do something.

I spat viciously into the gravel and slowly plucked a grass stalk to chew.

"I said commere, buddy, and I meant *commere*," I said quietly, lowering my eyes to slits. When he got closer I could tell that I was at least a head taller. Lawrence came right up to me as I sat there. I didn't look at him, I just stared out over his front lawn.

"That was my brother you hit with that rock," I began. He just grinned and stood there in the driveway. I watched him out of the corner of my eye. "I don't like people to go around hitting my brother with rocks. I don't like it, see?"

That's when he clouted me with the two-by-four.

"Are you all right, Bud?" inquired Caleb. He was propping me back up against the garage and I could feel a great big tight lump forming on my forehead.

"Yeah, I'm all right," I said, trying to see through the haze that had suddenly come between our house and the one next door. "Where'd he go?" I asked Caleb.

"He beat it back into his house right after he hit you," said Caleb. "I was watching through the garage window. I wanted to watch you take him."

Just then we heard a screen door slam, and

the man with the moustache came barreling up to the hedge. The way he stood there, looking over at us, made his moustache look like it grew right up out of the hedge and into his nose.

"You two," he shouted at me and Caleb, "had better not hit Lawrence with sticks again! You hear me? You two bother him again and I'll call a policeman and have you put in jail. And I'll tell your papa, too."

You could tell by the way he said it that he thought "telling your papa" was much worse than going to jail.

Me and Caleb just froze there, with our eyes bugged out, while that man let us have it.

"And," he shouted, "don't go breaking any more of my elm trees!"

"We didn't —" I started to say, but the moustache and the man on the other end of it were steaming back to the new house.

"Little Lawrence is smart, too," Caleb said respectfully.

"Not only is he smart, he's the biggest liar in Harleyville since you won the championship," I answered.

To say that we kept away from our new neighbors for the next few days is putting it mildly. Lawrence had really put the buffalo on me and Caleb. We wouldn't go near that garage. In fact, we spent most of our time up in our room wondering how we could get back in power.

"I give up," I said, one afternoon, several days later. Caleb stood over by the window, looking out toward the new house.

"Me too," he said. "And just look at that sister of his, throwing her ball around out there, just asking us to come outside and get massacred by that little terror. Why, I haven't seen him for three or four days now, but I know darn well he's hiding over there somewhere, just waiting for you and me to come outside."

"Hey, wait a minute!" I said.

"Yeah?" said Caleb.

"Amos! Wasn't Amos getting back from YMCA Camp last night?"

"Let's see; yesterday was the twenty-third — yeah, that was when he was supposed to get back," said Caleb.

"Well, let's get him on the phone. Tell him to come right over. He'll have to come right by the new house. And little Lawrence will be right there waiting for some nice fresh meat."

I called Amos up, and Amos said he'd be right over. I knew he would; Amos Finch is one of my best friends, along with Dink Fowler.

We waited by the window for the show. Pretty soon we saw Amos coming down the street, whistling and kicking a can ahead of him. That pretty girl heard him too and came right out to see who it was.

"Now he'll get it," I told Caleb.

But Lawrence didn't jump out from the bushes with a rock or anything, like I'd hoped he would.

"Where did he go?" asked Caleb.

"I don't know," I answered. And Amos and that pretty girl played ball together for most of the morning. I could have shot myself.

"Come on, let's go," I said finally. Me and Caleb made our way to the side yard where Amos and that girl were playing.

"I've got to go inside now, Amos," she was saying, "but I can come out for a while after supper." She smiled at him and ignored us before disappearing inside the house.

Amos strolled over like the cat that had swallowed the canary.

"That's my new girl," he announced proudly. "Some looker, huh?"

"She tell you about her brother yet?" I asked him.

"She doesn't have a brother," Amos replied.

"That's what you think," said Caleb. "Just wait until you meet Lawrence."

"Oh, you mean Lawrence," said Amos. "She told me about him. She hates him. He's her cousin from St. Louis. Just visited her for a few days. She's been bored sick ever since he left. You should have helped her kill some time, Bud," said Amos, winking at me.

 **6**

I never will understand why grown-ups are so surprised on the morning after Halloween to wake up and find everything gone haywire. If they were half awake the week before, they would have seen us boys getting ready. Most of them don't even know it's Halloween until they read it the following morning in the paper.

We usually started our preparations about a week before Halloween. It takes a little bit of planning to cause all the confusion that we do. We like to play a good joke on people. Nothing permanent or destructive, but something that is funny, when it happens to the right person. Anyway, that last week in October was a busy one for me and Caleb and the friends we hung around with.

On Halloween night we all met, with Clint and Myron and a lot of other kids, over behind school.

"Everybody got what they're supposed to have?" whispered Myron.

We all said "Yeah!" in the crisp darkness.

"Okay. Then let's split up and do our different jobs. Remember, back here at nine-thirty. And don't anybody be late! If you get here early, just lie low in these bushes. Don't make any racket, or we'll all get caught. And by nine-thirty things ought to be popping around here pretty good."

Earlier in the week, me and Caleb and Dink had been assigned the two blocks on Kimbrough Street, just north of Main Street, and that's where we went, as fast as we could. Seeing all the other groups heading off on their own missions gave us a feeling of being a part of some big scheme, like in a war or something.

Our area was made up of old two-story houses, sitting back from the street a good long way. There were a lot of big maples and elms, which were supposed to provide us with some cover.

"Just look at all those cars parked along the street!" commented Caleb hungrily, as we got to the start of our territory.

"You wait till I whistle, hear?" I asked. "I'll get caught for certain if you start too soon."

"Sure," said Caleb. "I'll wait until I hear you whistle."

We three split up, as I imagined all the other groups doing at about that same time. It must have been just a few minutes after eight.

I started at the end of the street and began painting doorknobs with the bacon grease I had swiped from the icebox. I had to be careful, because most folks would be listening for trick-or-treaters on their front porches; but I'd worn rubber-soled shoes for just that reason.

The first two houses went fine; I left the doorknobs thick and gooey with old bacon grease. I was just finishing off the third when I heard steps behind me. I hadn't expected them at all, and I'll admit I almost chucked that grease can and lit out for home.

Instead, I went over the railing on one side of the porch. I hit the ground as soft and quiet as a baked yam. The footsteps walked right by where I'd been, and I just froze to the ground and listened.

Knock-knock-knock.

Pause. Heavy feet moving through the house.

"Yes?" I recognized the voice of Mr. Swarthope, who was the dispatcher at Harry Mangus's lumberyard. Everybody said he had a temper like a crazy man. I wished I'd run on home after all.

"Twick or Tweat!" said some little kid.

"Well," said Mr. Swarthope, "I'll treat, all right. I don't want to get tricked."

He went back inside the house for a minute, while the kiddies waited at the door.

"Here you are," said Mr. Swarthope, but I had no idea what he was putting in their paper bags. "Don't forget now," he called after them as they were leaving, "I've treated you — no tricks now! No soap on the windows."

"No, sir," yelled a little voice from the sidewalk.

That's when Mr. Swarthope put his hand on the outside of the doorknob and started to go back inside.

"What the Sam Hill is this?" he muttered to himself. There was a long pause, while he must have stood there and looked at his hand. "How do you like those little hellions, Edith?" he said to someone inside the house. "I give them candy, and they plaster nasty stuff all over my doorknob! I hope that taffy pulls out every tooth in their mean little heads!"

I lay low until I was sure he had really gone inside, and then I took off for the next house. I got all the rest of the houses on that side of the street without any trouble. Then I started down the other side.

I had gotten about half of the other houses done when a great big cocker spaniel came leaping out at me from the driveway between two houses. He barked like I was stealing something.

"Hello, Burt," I said, as nice as I knew how. "Nice old Burt. Good old doggie." It calmed him down some, but the lights on the front porch went on, and I knew if I ran, old Burt would bite a hole in me without batting an eye.

Mrs. Filgerson walked out on her porch and looked at me standing there in her front yard, hiding the can of grease behind my back. Burt was standing right next to me, pointing.

"Why, Bud Wallings! What is it? Come back, Burt, it's all right," she said.

"That sure is a fine old dog, Mrs. Filgerson," I remarked. "He sure is a good old watchdog, all right."

"What were you doing, Bud?" she asked me.

"Oh, I was just . . . just walking by, taking my little brother trick-or-treating. He's too young to go by himself, you know." I smiled, sweet as cotton candy.

"Well, where is he? Bring him on in. I have lots of goodies, and your mother told me all about that clown costume she was making him. She said something about an Indian costume for you . . ."

"Uhh . . . yes, ma'am. I tore it on a nail. And Caleb, why he's down at Mr. Swarthope's right now, singing some songs he learned at

Sunday School just for Mr. Swarthope. Mr. Swarthope just loves to hear Caleb sing."

"Well, bring him on by here, when he gets through," she insisted. "I must see that clown suit."

"Oh, yes, ma'am. I sure will," I said.

"Come on inside, Burt. You should know better than to snap at children out trick-or-treating," she said. Burt gave me one look that told me he knew darn well I wasn't doing any trick-or-treating with that can of bacon fat behind my back, but he went inside.

I thought she had me on those costumes. Mama had made them for us and of course we had ditched them in the garage as soon as we got outside.

I finished my job in a cold sweat, but anyhow, I finished.

When I was done, I carefully stashed my tools in the hollow of an old elm tree that stood on the corner. Then I puckered up and whistled, twice long and one short. Then I waited.

Caleb had heard me all right.

Way down at the other end of the street, an automobile horn began to honk. Not off and on, but steady. Caleb was wedging sticks between the front seats and the horns. Soon there was another horn, accompanying the first one. And in a minute there was one more.

It seemed to me he was moving too slow, that people in the first house would be out and after him before he had finished the street. I could just picture my little brother in jail.

But when he got to the middle of the block, Caleb must have figured the same thing. All of a sudden it seemed like the whole sky was full of automobile horns honking all together, like a glee club with cars, and each one was singing a different note.

Down the block, porch lights began to go on, and I could just barely see people running back and forth between the street and their houses.

"That does it," said Caleb, puffing up beside me. He threw himself down on the ground and tried to catch his breath.

"What took you so long?" I asked him.

"Had (puff-puff-puff), had to lock them (puff-puff), so they couldn't get in and (puff-puff), take the sticks out too soon."

"So that's what they were running back to the houses for, the keys!" I said.

"Yeah. And it was right about nine o'clock, too, wasn't it? I was on time?" he asked.

"I think so. We better start back, before somebody starts looking for us," I said.

"What about Dink? Don't we get to stick around and watch him throw those rotten apples down from that tree he's hidden in?"

"No! Don't you remember? He's got to stay there until things quiet down again. We've got to hurry."

I had thought that when we got away from our area we would get away from those auto horns too, but it didn't happen that way. All over town the same things were happening, and some different things too.

We crept toward school through the backyards, because there was too much activity in the streets by now. Cars were driving up and down, and little knots of neighbors stood out under the streetlights, talking. I didn't want to know what they were saying.

We stopped in some bushes, next to a garage, where we could look out at the street. We were behind McLeod's old house. He was the one that used to shoot a BB gun at any dog who wandered onto his precious lawn. He might have been the one who poisoned Petunia.

The unlucky thing about Mr. McLeod was that he happened to have a fireplug in front of his house.

Right then, that fireplug looked like Old Faithful on a rampage. Water was shooting thirty feet in the air, and huge sloppy puddles were beginning to form all around the house. McLeod was out in front, trying to cap the hydrant with a garbage can lid. As we watched, he darted in and tried to force that lid down on the spouting water.

"Look, Caleb!" I said. "Look at Mr. McLeod."

"Wow," said Caleb. "Right up in the air."

"Clint did a good job with that fireplug wrench, didn't he?" I added.

"He sure did!"

The water was climbing up over the curb by now, because some naughty children or somebody had stuffed up the drain in front of McLeod's with paper boxes. Oh, it was like a circus, getting through Harleyville that night.

One time we looked out and saw about twelve automobile tires rolling down Kimbrough Street, without a sign of a car on top of them. Dogs were barking everywhere, and great gangs of little children were moving up and down the sidewalk, singing and eating their loot.

When we finally got back, almost all the different groups were already in. The group leaders had to report to Clint, to tell him how well things had gone, and I reported for us, since Dink was still up in that tree. When the last bunch of commandos had checked in, Clint told us to separate and get home, fast and quiet, as the whole town would lynch us if they caught anybody. And I believe they would have, too.

"Oh, and Harvey?" asked Clint. "How's your garbage thrower?" Harvey Willis had built a gadget, powered by a stretched inner tube, that could throw a wet bag of garbage seventy-five feet or so.

"I think I got her fixed, now," said Harvey.

"You still got that wagon full of garbage?" asked Clint.

"Yep," said Harvey, proudly. "But I didn't get a chance to fire a single shot."

"Well, take it on home and get rid of it. It's too late to use it now."

"Okay," Harvey sighed. He walked home with me and Caleb, since he lived in our direction. We made it safely back to our house, and Harvey came into the garage with us while we put on our costumes again.

"You're not really gonna wear those things?" Harvey asked us.

"Yeah, we've got to," I said. "Our mama thinks we were out trick-or-treating tonight."

"You were tricking, all right. Boy, I wish I'd gotten to use my catapult. It worked perfect all afternoon."

"Hey," said Caleb. "There's somebody out in our backyard."

We looked, and sure enough, there was a moving shadow down by my big oak tree. It seemed to be motioning us, so we went down there, quiet as hungry roaches. It was Myron Webster.

"Listen," he said, sounding worried. "I just came from Kimbrough Street. It's really something down there."

"You betcha it is!" smiled Caleb.

"Dink's caught up in that tree. All the neighbors have their lights on and are standing around outside. He can't get down."

"What'll we do?" asked Harvey.

"You still got your machine?" asked Myron.

"Sure," said Harvey.

"Let's go," said Myron.

"What about these?" I said, pointing to those stupid outfits that me and Caleb had just finished putting back on.

"Haven't got time to change now. Let's go!" said Myron.

We snuck through the backyards to the scene of the crime. Some of those car horns were still blowing; their owners must not have been home or something, and the neighbors couldn't unlock the doors to stop that honking. They were beginning to act kind of nervous, and some of them were holding their ears.

"Which tree is Dink in?" asked Harvey.

"That one," said Caleb. He really looked nutty in that clown suit.

"I think I've got it!" said Myron. "Look, Bud, you and Caleb, in your costumes, try to draw everybody's attention over to the other side of the street. When you get a crowd, I'll signal Dink, and he can slip down and back here. Harvey, load up that cannon and be ready to cover us if we should have to retreat in a hurry."

"I'm not going anywhere in this crazy Indian get-up," I announced.

"Me neither," Caleb agreed.

"You've got to," said Myron. "If Dink doesn't get down, his mother'll start looking for him and the apple cart will be tipped. You've just got to do it," he repeated. From the way he said it, I realized that we really did.

"Come on, Caleb," I said. I'd have rather walked right up that elm tree and taken Dink's place than to go out on that busy street in that silly uniform. But it had to be done.

We made it out to the street without anybody noticing us. We went right straight across, like we were just kids looking for an apple or some candy. We stopped in front of Mrs. Filgerson's house. All the neighbors started watching us. I felt scared. They all stopped talking and just looked at us.

"Hello, Mrs. Filgerson," said Caleb. "House-cleaning?"

Mrs. Filgerson had been working on her doorknob with a damp cloth.

"No, I'm not housecleaning," she said bitterly. For a minute, I thought she might be planning on throwing that rag at us. "Some bad boys came to my house and put something smelly on my doorknob. You two wouldn't know anything about that, would you?"

"Oh, no, ma'am," I insisted. "I been home getting that nail hole sewn up, so I could show my costume to you." Caleb looked at me like he thought I was crazy. "See, Mrs. Filgerson, I'm an Indian!" I whooped and hollered a little, hoping to show all those neighbors that were watching us that I had the true Halloween spirit.

"My, my," said Caleb. "I didn't know you were so talented, Bud."

"Shut up!" I whispered. "I brought Caleb to show you his costume too, Mrs. Filgerson. See him? This is Caleb, you know, my little brother. He's a clown, Mrs. Filgerson. See all those spots?"

"Yes, I see them," she said. She was still suspicious, and I think the rest of the neighbors were too. "Come up here on the porch and let me have a look at those costumes. If you boys were really just trick-or-treating, I owe you an apology. *Some* little devils did all kinds of things around here."

We went up on the porch, and she looked at each of our booby suits.

"Sing some songs for Mrs. Filgerson, Caleb, like you did for Mr. Swarthope," I prompted. I was afraid she'd ask him about it, and he wouldn't know.

"Do *what*?" asked Caleb.

"You know, Caleb," I said, trying to laugh. "Sing some of those cute songs you're always learning at Sunday School."

Caleb just looked at me. He was very angry.

"Little ones to him belong. They are weak, but he is strong," sang Caleb, looking at his goofy pointed clown shoes.

"That's all right, Caleb," said Mrs. Filgerson. "Your voice must be tired from singing so much tonight."

"Yes, it sure is, isn't it, Caleb?" I said. "Well, we better be going, Mrs. Filgerson," I said. "Mama might begin to worry about us. I just wanted you to see our pretty costumes that our mama made us."

"Good night, boys," said Mrs. Filgerson. As we left, the rest of the neighbors closed in around her, and over my shoulder I could hear her telling them that we couldn't possibly have had anything to do with all those pranks along Kimbrough Street. I was glad she hadn't remembered to give us any treats, because I felt kind of mean telling her all those lies.

We walked straight up the sidewalk, so we wouldn't draw any attention to where Myron and Dink were hiding. We'd just made the turn at the corner when we heard an awful yell from down the block. It was all we needed to send us on our way, fast.

We waited in the little park at the end of Rainwater Street, and sure enough, it wasn't long before three dark figures slipped across the road and started down toward our house.

"Over here!" I whispered, as loud as I dared.

The three of them joined us immediately. They were puffing so hard that they couldn't talk for a little while.

"What was that yell we heard?" I asked Myron Webster, after I'd given him a moment to catch his breath.

"McLeod. It was McLeod," said Myron, holding his sides. "He was the only one that saw Dink coming down, and he followed him into his backyard."

"Then what happened?" Caleb wanted to know.

"He got my catapult!" grinned Harvey, but for some reason, he didn't seem too disappointed.

"You should have seen him!" said Dink, laughing. "You just should have seen McLeod."

"Why?" I asked.

"We had to leave it and run," said Harvey. "My catapult. And the wagon, loaded with garbage. He got them both."

"Don't worry, Harvey," said Dink. "You can have my old wagon, for saving my life."

"Old Harv let McLeod come in until he wasn't more than twenty feet away," said Myron. "He fired that contraption and about five pounds of wet coffee grounds and banana peels and egg shells caught McLeod right smack between the nose and the chin."

"No fooling?" I asked.

"Right on the old button!" agreed Dink. "He just stood there and spit coffee grounds for a few seconds. And then he yelled like a crazy man and started after us."

"Could he see anybody?" asked Caleb.

"Naw," said Harvey. "It was too dark."

We busted up for home then, and me and Caleb got a lecture for being forty-five minutes late. Papa asked us if we knew who might have poured syrup in our mailbox, but of course we didn't have any idea who it was.

"Come here a minute, Bud," Papa asked, just as we started up to bed. "Let me see your hands."

I had to show them to him. They were all greasy.

"Good night boys," said Papa. "See you in the morning."

And the next day there were all sorts of stories in the paper about flooded conditions in certain parts of town, and about people who got hit with rotten apples. And one gentleman over on Kimbrough Street was even hit in the face with "flying debris" launched by some kind of machine that was now in the hands of the police.

"Many cases of greased doorknobs were also reported," concluded Papa, reading from the paper. He looked up at me. "Next time, get that stuff off before you come inside," he said, winking at me.

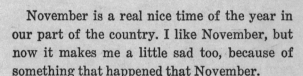

7

November is a real nice time of the year in our part of the country. I like November, but now it makes me a little sad too, because of something that happened that November.

Along about the middle of the month the first frost usually sets in around Harleyville. When you get out of town, into the country, on a blue-sky day, with just enough wind to rustle the few leaves still clinging to the trees, why then you're in the middle of something that can't be described or photographed or anything, it's so pretty. The cover grass in the woods is brittle and brown like ashes that disintegrate wherever you put your foot. And the cold, pure, clean air goes right into your muscles and bones when you breathe it.

There's really nothing like walking through the woods in autumn. It makes you so happy inside, you feel like busting. But you can't talk about it to your friends, or even your family.

You've just got to get out there *in* it and feel the sadness and prettiness of it; and when you go home, somehow, it's like you've just come from church.

When that first frost comes along, it takes the pollen out of the air so that the dogs can scent quail, and Papa usually takes off from work a couple of times a week to go hunting.

One night, right after supper, he was telling us about his day's hunt.

"Greg's little pointer, Lou," Papa was saying, "went down on a point right by the truck as we came back through Old Man Green's barn lot. We already had —"

"Papa?" interrupted Caleb. "Papa, when can me and Bud go hunting?"

"That's right, Papa," I added quickly, before he had a chance to answer.

"Well, uh . . ." said Papa.

"You promised us last year, but you forgot about it until it was too late," argued Caleb.

"You did, Papa," I reminded him. "You said we could take our twenty-twos and hunt squirrels in that big hickory grove down at Gramps'."

"I promised you, huh? Well, I guess this weekend's as good as any," he said.

"Yippee!" hollered me and Caleb.

And that Saturday we must have been awake at dawn. We were lying on our beds already dressed when Papa stuck his head in our room.

"Time t'get up, boys," he said. His eyes were still closed, and he looked like he was still asleep.

"We're ready, Papa, whenever you are."

"Humh?" said Papa, opening his eyes. "Oh. Fine."

A few minutes later we were in the front seat of Papa's car heading out in the country toward Gramps' farm. Papa had fixed us toast and jelly for breakfast. He just drank coffee.

At the last minute, Weenie and Petunia had climbed into the car, and we had to take time out to put Petunia back inside the house. Weenie crawled under the front seat, where we couldn't get him out, so we had to let him come along.

"We'll leave him with Gramps," said Papa.

The sun was just beginning to make the sky glow, up above the horizon in the east. There was a thin film of clouds over where the sun was coming up, and it began to turn painful red and purple colors as it got to be dawn. The cold air was sharp, and you could see your breath.

The sun was just clearing the earth when we got to Gramps'. He had been expecting us, and so there was a pot of hot coffee waiting. Even me and Caleb got to drink some, with lots of milk and sugar in it. Gramps wasn't going with us, as he had all his farm chores to attend to.

"Now, boys, here's the way we'll work it," began Papa, after he threw down the last part of his black coffee and chunked the big white mug down on the kitchen table. We'd taken our guns out of their cases and put our coats and caps back on, all ready to go. Weenie had crawled out of the car and was scurrying around the kitchen like he planned on going too.

"When you hear a noise, stop. Listen, and try to figure out what it is and where it's coming from. If it's a squirrel, one of us will go around on one side of the tree, and the squirrel will keep on the far side of the tree from him. Get it? That will make a good shot for the other two. If you see any squirrels running, *don't* shoot at them. You couldn't hit them anyway, and you could hit a cow or a pig or even some*body*. Keep those rifles on safety, and don't even chamber a round of ammunition until I say it's all right."

"What about Weenie?" asked Caleb.

"We'll leave him inside. I don't want to have to keep track of him too," said Papa. He glanced around the room to see if we had forgotten anything. "Let's go."

We started out in single file, walking along

a cow path toward the hickory grove. Papa led, and I was last. The sun was bright now, but it was still cold. The frost hung on the grass and leaves so that they didn't even crunch when you walked on them.

We walked a long way without saying anything. The woods were enough to absorb our thoughts. All about us lay the quiet, bright beauty of autumn.

As I was walking along, I began to notice noises behind me, breathing sounds, and the sound of soft, careful footpads in the leaves. When I turned around, I wasn't really too surprised to see Weenie.

He had gotten out of Gramps' house somehow and was following along as quietly as he knew how. When I looked at him, he whined softly and then rolled over on his back and pawed the air. He knew that he should have been at home in the first place, but he just couldn't stand it. He had *had* to come hunting with us.

"Beat me," his eyes seemed to say, "kick me, do anything. But let me come along."

"Papa?" I called.

Papa turned around.

"What? Oh, for cat's sakes! Did that mutt follow us clear out here?"

"I guess he did," I answered, although it was pretty obvious.

"Well, he might as well tag along, now. We don't want to take the time to go back. If he starts barking when we get to the grove, I'm going to tie him in a knot around a tree somewhere," said Papa, but I don't think he really would have.

We went on, over hills and down through valleys until I didn't have any idea where we were. Weenie stayed at my heels, quiet as a long mouse. Finally, up ahead of us, I could see a patch of gold up in some tall trees that told me we were near the hickory grove.

"Now slow down!" whispered Papa. "We want to work up to it gradually."

When we got a little closer I heard a sound like a woodpecker, but I knew it was a squirrel somewhere up above us working on a hickory nut. Papa and Caleb heard it too, and Papa motioned me around to the left.

Carefully I circled around to the opposite side of the big tree Papa had pointed to. Looking back, I saw Caleb's red cap. He was aiming his rifle up in the tree, and Papa was standing right behind him, trying to help. I waited for a couple of minutes, and then BLAAM!

I crashed through the scrub toward them.

"Did you hit him, Caleb? Where's the squirrel?" I yelled.

"Naw, he missed," said Papa, disgustedly.

"He peeled bark about four feet over that squirrel and off to the left. How many times have I told you to squeeze that trigger, not try to jerk it off?"

"A whole lot of times, Papa," admitted Caleb.

"Where did that squirrel go, Papa? It's my shot next," I said.

"He's holed up by now," said Papa. "We'll keep moving."

Before long, we heard another noise like a woodpecker, and this time I saw him. He was sitting up on a high limb chewing on a hickory nut, making that funny noise.

I pointed, and everybody froze. Papa tiptoed over to me, and I sighted in. I could see that fat little rascal perched right on the end of my front sight as I pulled the trigger.

"You missed too," commented Papa.

We continued on through the woods, and after a while, Caleb shot him a squirrel. You'd have thought it was a moose or something, the way he went on. And it wasn't long until I got one too. By nine o'clock Papa had four gray squirrels in the game pocket of his coat.

"I think we've scared them all out of the grove, boys," said Papa, right after Caleb had killed number four with a real good kneeling shot. "Let's move along that creek bed and see if we find any more there."

The creek wound around like a crazy snake, and we walked along slowly beside it. Along both sides of the creek we began to run into little limestone cliffs that were from ten to twenty feet above the level of the water. But we didn't see any more squirrels.

We'd gone about half a mile, staying parallel to the creek, when we heard Weenie begin to bark some distance behind us. I hadn't even missed him.

"What's the matter with Weenie?" asked Caleb. "Why's he barking like that?"

Papa listened for a minute.

"If I didn't know better," said Papa, "I'd say that he was running a squirrel. That's the way a good hound sounds off, when he's close to one; but Weenie wouldn't know about that, being a town dog. I don't know what it is."

We kept listening, and the sounds came closer. Then we saw him. He was up on top of the hill, falling and rolling and yiping his way in hot pursuit of a red fox squirrel who was moving down that hill like a rat from a fire.

Weenie was pathetic, he was so excited. I guess he knew he might not ever again have a chance to run a squirrel in our direction. His long, awkward body was having quite a time getting over rocks and logs and things, but he managed to stay close to that squirrel through sheer determination.

"Well, bless him, boys! Will you look at there!" said Papa, surprised and kind of proud at the same time. "He's running that squirrel right to us, just like a real hunting dog would."

"It's my turn," I reminded him.

"Better let me have this one, Bud," said Papa. "He's moving too fast for you to hit with your twenty-two."

Swiftly Papa poked a shell into his twenty-gauge and waited. Sure enough, whenever the squirrel tried to turn off to the side, Weenie would let out a terrible series of yelps and that squirrel would straighten out almost immediately. They were both coming down that hill at full speed, and I suddenly noticed the little cliff that separated them from the creek. It was about fifteen feet high, and the creek bed below was all rock.

They kept coming, too, all eight of those little short legs moving like pistons. Papa cocked his shotgun and waited.

That squirrel had had a hard time maintaining a ten-foot lead; when he got to the ledge, there was no question about what he was going to do. He took a few fast steps and leaped out into nothing but clean, fall air, spreading the loose skin between his legs, like

91

he thought he was a glider. Papa had sighted in and caught him perfectly, in mid-air, about three feet above the creek bank.

But I had stopped watching the squirrel. I was watching Weenie, and so was Caleb. Poor Weenie had been going so fast he didn't have a chance in the world to stop before he got to the ledge.

Suddenly it was right before him. He tried hard to stop himself and slide down — I can still remember the puzzled look on his face — but it was too steep, and his momentum was too great.

He fell through the air silently, struggling to keep his feet beneath his body. Then he hit one of the big rocks in the creek bed and lay still.

"How was that shot?" asked Papa.

All I could do was point to the creek bed where Weenie lay.

"Good Lord!" said Papa, realizing what had happened for the first time. All three of us raced to the spot and got there at about the same time.

We could tell it was a bad accident for Weenie. His front paws were crumpled beneath him, and his long, funny body was bent all wrong. Papa tried to feel his back, and Weenie turned his head around slowly, and licked Papa's hand. You could tell it hurt Weenie to move.

"It's broken," said Papa.

Me and Caleb looked at each other and then back to Papa. Papa wouldn't look at us.

"Can the vet fix it, Papa?" asked Caleb. "I'll carry him back to the car." Caleb looked funny and pale; all of a sudden I felt the same way.

"No, Caleb," said Papa. Weenie laid his head down in Papa's hand and whined, real quietly. And then me and Caleb knew.

"Start on back," said Papa, quietly. "Give me your twenty-two before you go, Bud."

I was frozen there, and Caleb looked at me with big eyes. I thought about all the times I'd used Weenie for a pillow in front of the fireplace reading the comics, and I knew that Papa had just started to love Weenie this morning, when he saw him chasing that red squirrel.

Papa was reaching out for me to give him my rifle.

"I'll do it, Papa," I said.

Papa looked at me kind of funny — like he didn't understand at first, and then like he thought more of me for saying it.

"You better let me," he said.

"I want to," I said. "I know him better than you do."

"All right," said Papa. "We'll wait for you back in the grove."

Weenie hurt bad. He wanted to try to get up and walk away from the pain, but his hind legs wouldn't move, and he didn't understand. He looked up at me as Caleb and Papa started to walk away, like he wanted me to help him get up and go too.

I smoothed his coat the best I could before I chambered the little twenty-two shell and took off the safety. I could feel Weenie's muzzle warm in my hand, but I couldn't see him very well.

Caleb and Papa were waiting for me in the grove.

"He was brave," I told them. "He was very brave."

 **8**

Early in December, when it was too early to start whooping it up for Christmas and too late to plan anything for Thanksgiving, me and Dink Fowler and Amos Finch were asked to join a club that some other boys from our school were starting. Our club was called "693402."

We called it that because it sounded official and kind of mysterious, like a code. Actually, that number had no meaning whatever, and those that weren't in the club spent a good many painful hours trying to figure what 693402 could mean. We planned it that way.

Clint Harker, who was in eighth grade, was the one who thought of it. Me and Dink and Amos were the only ones from our grade who were asked to join. It didn't hurt our standing any, either.

We met after school on Wednesdays in a field right next to school but hidden from any nosy teachers by several big clumps of sumac bushes.

Me and Dink and Amos were called Bird-dogs, because we were youngest and supposed to be the worst stinkers. Eighth graders were called Hounds, which was a whole lot better than Birddogs, but not near so good as the club officers, who were called Emperors. We Birddogs always got the dirty jobs, no matter what it was, and we had to mind the Hounds and Emperors and do what they told us to, or we'd get kicked out of the club. We couldn't even come into the meetings until all the Emperors and Hounds had taken their seats.

"Let the Birddogs enter!" yelled Myron Webster, who was Chief Assassin. That meant he could pick on us Birddogs whenever he felt like. He felt like it a lot, too.

We three came in, solemn as saints, and sat down on the ground, filling in the weakest spots in the circle around the Chief Assassin and Clint Harker, who was President.

"Birddogs all present and accounted for, Sir Chief Assassin," said Dink, gravely. Dink was kind of King of us Birddogs.

"Allah permit that your guts not rot on the desert," prayed the Sir Chief Assassin, who had written the dialogue for these meetings himself.

"All members present or accounted for,

Holy President," Myron said to Clint. He got down on his knees and bowed until Clint touched him on the nose with the little finger of his right hand. That meant Myron could stand up again, which he did, immediately.

"Tell all 693402's to rise for the Oath!" commanded Clint.

"Rise, Emperors. Rise, Hounds. Rise, Birddogs, for the Oath of the Clan!" said Myron, like he was leading a revival or something.

Then we all stood up and held our two fists up even with our eyes and looked at them. We didn't just *look* at our fists, we were supposed to *stare* at them.

"Our right fist to the blood of our enemy, our left fist to eternal victory!" we all said together, like the pledge of allegiance. We didn't have any enemies for our right fists yet, but we expected some at any time.

Then we sat back down on the ground.

"What's new?" Clint asked Myron.

"Oh, nothing," Myron answered. "It's just Wednesday. That's the day we're supposed to meet."

"Don't we have anything to talk about?" said Clint.

"Nope. Amos Finch paid his dues, and that's all we talked about at the last meeting. Unless you've thought up something for the Birddogs to do. They want to try and become Hounds and have to do something to prove themselves worthy," said Myron. I guess if we'd have had some other kind of business to attend to, the whole thing never would have come up. But since we didn't have any more business, we Birddogs caught it head-on.

"Yeah!" grinned Clint. "I remember now. They have to do something brave before they can become Hounds, don't they?"

"Yep," said Myron. "Got any ideas?"

"I sure do," said Clint. "Rise, Birddogs, and hear the words of your leader."

We Birddogs all rose, like we were on wires or something.

"On the eighth day of this month, when the moon is at its fullest, you three will proceed to the old Stapleton farmhouse, at midnight, and once there, you will go directly to the attic of the house, where, you will remember, Old Man Stapleton was found, hanging from a rafter by his neck with his tongue stuck out of his mouth in death!"

He didn't have to say that last part. Just to mention the old Stapleton place gave me the screaming willies, and the way Clint talked about it made me want to forget all about ever becoming a Hound.

"When you get there, you will rip loose one of the old swallows' nests up in the attic and, with a jackknife, you will prick your fingers, and all three of you will spill your blood into that swallow's nest. Then you will return to your homes and bring the nest with you to the next meeting to prove you actually did it. Do you understand?"

Clint looked up and down all three of us, just daring anyone to whine about what we had to do.

"We understand, O Holy President, and it shall be done!" said that jerk, Dink.

"The Oath, then," said Clint.

"Our right fist to the blood of our enemy, our left fist to eternal victory!" everybody sang out.

We three Birddogs left together. Later, after it was all over, I found out what the rest of 693402 did after we'd gone; they made plans to rig our assignment on us, as you will see.

But we didn't know anything about it at the time.

The eighth was Saturday, and it was on us before we knew it. Amos had gotten permission to spend the night at Dink's house. Dink's parents were in Queenston for the weekend, but his older sister was supposed to be looking after him and Amos. By eleven o'clock that night she was snoring like a freight train on an uphill climb, and they took off.

I had a little more trouble than that. Caleb

had sensed that something was up, and he stuck to me like flypaper in a windstorm. I snuck up to bed while he was still fighting the idea, though, and pretended to be asleep when he came in.

I lay there nervously and waited for the house to quiet down. In a little while I heard Papa switch off the light in his and Mama's room. Callie's room was downstairs, so I didn't have to worry about her. I waited a few more minutes and then slowly sat up in bed.

"Where you going, Bud?" whispered Caleb.

"Pulling up my blanket — you mind?"

"Oh. No, go right ahead."

"Thanks," I replied. It worried me that Caleb was so jumpy. I had slipped into bed with my clothes on so I could slip out quietly without him waking up; but if he didn't drop off to sleep soon, I'd be too late to meet Dink and Amos.

At last his breathing came more evenly and he seemed to be asleep. I carried my shoes and jacket over to the window, unlatched the storm window, and climbed out on the porch roof and down my oak tree.

Dink and Amos were waiting for me beside the lumber yard fence.

"Man, it's a cold one!" muttered Dink, as we left. "You've got that flashlight, Bud?"

"Yeah. I've got it all right," I said.

"I got the jackknife, too," added Amos.

Stapleton's old farmhouse stood out of town about a mile or so, along an old dirt road that nobody used any more. Old Man Stapleton had been a prosperous merchant in the "good old days" of Harleyville, when the railroad had made it a lot more important city than it is today. Stapleton's wife and daughter had both died of the scarlet fever, one winter, and they had found the old man about a week later, hanging up there in the attic, swinging back and forth with the breeze that blew in from under the eaves.

All the trees and bushes had grown up around the old place, and it had gradually earned the title of being haunted. It was the roosting place for all the swallows in Ogano County. The paint was all peeling off the old boards, and the porch floor was giving way the last time I'd been out there, which was at high noon one summer day, on our way to the creek. Other than for good old 693402, you wouldn't have gotten me near that place at night for love, money, or applesauce.

The night was still and cold, with a bright moon that made you shiver every time you looked at it. The trees and bushes were so quiet it was like they were frozen stiff, and whenever you talked or breathed, a great cloud of white smoke would come out of your mouth.

When we turned off onto the little lane that ran down to the Stapleton place, we could see the old buildings, dark shadows in the broken patches of moonlight. It was quiet as a coffin and twice as scary.

Me and Amos huddled on either side of Dink. You might say we tried to surround him. This kind of thing never seemed to bother Dink, and me and Amos were counting on him for a good bit of our courage. We crouched down and looked at the old farmhouse.

It was a two-story frame building that once must have been the rage of the country. A wide front porch ran the whole length of the place, and the high-pitched roof reminded us of the big attic that was up there, and what had been found inside, once, so long ago.

"The heck with it," whispered Amos. "Let's start our own club."

"Shh!" ordered Dink. "What do you mean? Let those guys know we're chicken-livered? Not me!"

Whatever Dink decided, I knew he spoke for all three of us; me and Amos weren't just about to leave him and go back down that dark road by ourselves.

"I can't tell if the front door is still on or not," mused Dink.

"It is," I answered him. "It's in the shadows. But that porch floor is giving way with termites."

"Better find another way in, then," Dink muttered. He thought about this for a minute. "Tell you what; let's shinny up that old tree beside the house. We can get in through the second-story window easy from there. We'll stick to the scrub and bushes. And let's keep it quiet!"

"Yeah," said Amos. "Except for my teeth chattering and my knees knocking." His face looked about the color of the moon, and I guess mine did too. Inside of me I was so scared I roared with noise, and yet on the outside you couldn't have heard me, or any of us, move across that yard and up that tree, unless you had special senses.

Dink climbed right up and made it through the window without a sound. The glass had all been broken out long ago, so we didn't have to worry about getting cut. Amos followed Dink up the tree and I wasn't far behind. Carefully we climbed over the sill and stood inside the dark, mouldy-smelling old building.

"I can't see anything," complained Amos. "Where are we?"

"Must be a bedroom," suggested Dink. "Let's

just stand here for a minute and let our eyes get used to the dark."

I blinked a few times and waited for something to happen. It did.

Suddenly Amos began to gurgle, deep down in his throat. His face seemed to glow sickly in the darkness.

"What is it?" I whispered.

He couldn't, or didn't, answer. He just pointed to the window. Me and Dink turned to look.

Just even with the bedroom window was a fork in the main branches of the tree. Crouching there was a dark shadow. The moonlight shone down through the branches on a small, scowling face that peered into the darkness where we stood.

"It's . . . it's Stapleton's little girl!" moaned Amos, finding his voice at last. "The one that died of scarlet fever. She don't want us here."

"No, it ain't," said Dink, disgustedly. He turned to me. "It's your little brother. He must have followed us."

"Caleb?" said Amos.

"That's the one," sighed Dink. "Come on, we better haul him in before he falls out of that tree on his head or something."

"But the Club!" I whispered. "The Club secrets. He'll find out our mission, and we'll all get kicked out."

"Can't help it now," said Dink. He leaned out the window, and for a minute I thought Caleb was going over backwards.

"That you, Bud?" he demanded quietly. "I can't see you, it's so dark. Is that you?"

"No, it ain't Bud," snarled Dink. "Now take my arm and climb in here before you fall."

"Oh. Hi, Dink," said Caleb, all smiles. He crawled in beside us. "Hello, Amos. Hi, Bud."

"When I get home . . ." I started to say, but Caleb interrupted me.

"I won't tell anybody, honest. I'll even help," he pleaded. "What do we do?"

"Oh, shut up and let's get going!" said Dink.

We tiptoed slowly out of the room and into the hall.

"Watch where you walk, and try to find a way to the attic," commanded Dink. Since he seemed to know what he was doing, we did what he said.

"There she is!" hissed Caleb. With the moonlight that shined in through the windows we could see him pointing at a dark spot on the hall ceiling. "It's a trap door," he explained. "We got one like that at our house."

Me and Dink and Amos looked at Caleb with surprised respect.

So far everything had gone okay, and Caleb's arrival had somehow calmed us down some. I was just beginning to feel like I might come out of this alive, when we heard this noise.

It seemed to come from down underneath us somewhere, but I might have been wrong. What made it so bad was that it was the noise somebody might make when they're choking.

"It's Old Man Stapleton!" moaned Amos. "He's up there swinging from a rafter, waiting for somebody to cut him down."

"Shh!" ordered Dink. I was so scared I couldn't have said persimmon pie, and Caleb seemed paralyzed.

We stood there, frozen, and listened for a long time. The house was as quiet as a school-yard on the fourth of July. Once we thought we heard a board squeak downstairs, and another time, something like a faraway belch.

"Just a possum or something," reasoned Dink. "He's rooting away down there for something." He acted like he heard noises like that every day.

"You ever heard a possum belch?" inquired Amos.

"No," admitted Dink. "But I guess they do, when there isn't anybody around."

"Well, there isn't gonna be anybody around, the next time he does that," warned Amos.

"Let's go," said Dink. "We've come this far. We can't quit now!"

I'll never know where he got the strength or

the nerve, but Dink jumped up and got his hands over the edge of that opening to the attic. Then he pulled himself the rest of the way up and disappeared into the blackness.

A rustling noise filtered down from the opening. Me and Caleb and Amos just looked at each other.

"Ssst!" came a noise from over our heads. "Grab my arm. I'll help pull you up." We could just barely make out Dink's face in the great cave above us.

"Go ahead, Amos," I said politely.

"After you, Bud," he replied.

When I swung myself up into the attic, I was sure I didn't want to stay. The boards were knocked out at one end, and outlined against the bright moonlight something that looked like a human body was hanging!

"Let go of my arm!" I ordered Dink. "I'm getting out of here!"

"Hold on!" said Dink. "Can't you see it?"

"You bet your life I see it," I said. "I seen it enough already to last me the rest of my life, however long that is."

"It's just a scarecrow. Myron and Clint must have swiped it out of somebody's cornfield and hung it up here to scare us," explained Dink.

"It is?" I asked. "Well, they sure succeeded."

"Hey! Don't leave us down here," Amos was

whispering, and we helped him and Caleb up. They reacted about the same way I had until Dink explained.

"And do you know what else?" Dink continued.

"I'd be afraid to guess," said Amos.

"I think," said Dink, "that those noises we heard was the rest of 693402 hiding downstairs to jump us when we came in through the front door. That's where they expected us, and they didn't see or hear us come in by that window."

"You really think so?" I asked.

"Sure, that's it. I should have guessed it before," said my smart friend Dink.

"What'll we do?" asked Amos.

"I'll tell you what we'll do," said Dink. "We'll fix those Hounds and Emperors good, since they don't know we're here."

"How'll we do that?" I asked.

"Well, to start with, let's get at them through the chimney. There's some bricks missing, and we can drop things down the flue so they'll make a big racket down in the living room. They're probably all standing there waiting for us to get here. That ought to get some action!"

We forgot about being scared, once we knew there was a chance to make our fellow members feel the same way we had. We searched the attic and found a few bricks and some small chunks of four-by-eight. Dink poked the bricks down the hole in the flue and let them go.

There must have been bottles or something in that fireplace, because we heard the crash all the way up in the attic.

And that's not all we heard.

Somebody downstairs just plain leaned back and hollered, like death was pulling at his innards.

"Cripes!" giggled Dink. "Listen to them, will you? They're scared silly!"

In a minute we heard steps on the stairs, fast steps. And then they were up on the second floor, running around from room to room like crazy people. The four of us sat on the very edge of the trap door and chuckled silently. Once in a while, somebody would zip by, right underneath us, without even thinking of looking up.

Dink was laughing so hard and having such a hard time staying quiet that the tears just rolled down his cheeks.

"Just wait till we see those guys at next Wednesday's meeting!" he whispered. "Just wait!"

Amos had been watching the vague figures

tear around beneath us. Suddenly he held up his hand for us to be quiet. Two of them had stopped right below us and were talking.

"Well, something had to make that racket. It didn't just happen, Harry," said a deep voice.

"I know, I know. But we've looked through the whole house. Whatever it was ain't here no more."

"Let's check the cellar again, Harry. We went through there pretty fast the first time." And then the two of them hurried toward the stairs.

Amos looked at us. He was very pale again. We listened to the footsteps die away.

"Uh . . . say, fellers," said Amos weakly. "We haven't got anybody in our club named Harry. Those were two grown men. They looked like railroad tramps to me."

We stared at each other. That weak feeling in my belly was back again, only worse.

"What'll we do?" I gulped.

"I'm the youngest," volunteered Caleb, like he was supposed to be saved first.

"We've got to get out!" whispered Dink. I think he was scared too, this time. "They'd fix us good for scaring them, if they caught us."

"They were going to the cellar," said Amos, suddenly. "We've got to go down now, if we want to get away. We've got to go quick! Before they finish looking in the cellar and come back upstairs."

We didn't waste any time getting out of that attic, but we were quiet about it. We tiptoed down the hall and followed right behind Dink as he carefully made his way down the creaky steps.

We could hear the voices of the two men down in the cellar, cussing each other and trying hard to find out what had scared them. At the bottom of the stairs we could see freedom, right out the front door, bathed in clear, liquid mooonlight. We gathered our strength to make the sprint through the yard and on back to Dink's house.

Just then, around the corner of the hall, not five feet from where we crouched on the stairs, came a fat old man with whiskers all over his face. He looked at us like he couldn't believe what he saw.

"Go like the dickens!" shouted Dink, diving out the door, with the three of us a half step behind him.

"H'yar they yare!" the old tramp yelled, as Caleb pushed past him.

"S'cuse me," said Caleb politely.

"Up h'yar!" shouted the tramp.

But we didn't stop to find out how fast his friends came up from the cellar. We lit out of there without taking time for a backward look.

I dodged into a clump of hickory scrub and was just beginning to wonder where the lane was when somebody grabbed me from behind and pinned my arms behind me. Two more somebodies came up out of the bushes in front of me. If I'd had a weak heart, I'd just be a name on a tombstone right now.

Somebody stuck their face up next to mine.

"Death to the Birddogs!" it said, and I recognized our Chief Assassin, Myron Webster.

"You guys sure took long enough," said Clint who was right behind Myron. "We almost froze out here, waiting to scare you. Did that scarecrow get you? And how'd you get in without us seeing you?"

Just then Dink crashed in on top of us. By then I'd almost caught my breath.

"Tramps!" I managed to say. "Tramps, back there in the house. They're after us."

"Huh?" frowned Myron.

"That's right," puffed Dink.

"Who's this?" Clint demanded, hauling Caleb into a patch of moonlight by one ear. Me and Dink just looked at each other. Caleb smiled weakly.

"That's my little brother, Caleb," I apologized.

"How do?" said Caleb.

"What's *he* doing here?" Myron wanted to know.

"He followed us," I explained. "He won't tell —"

"Where's Amos?" Clint suddenly interrupted.

We all looked at each other realized that Clint was right; Amos was missing.

Clint sized up the situation pretty fast; but then he's in eighth grade. "Come on, boys! Get some rocks and let's go!" he ordered.

Me and Dink and Caleb hooked onto the end of the gang. There must have been fifteen or twenty of us 693402's.

"Our right fist to the blood of our enemy, our left fist to eternal victory!" we shouted.

And then we made a wild rebel counterattack on the old Stapleton house. Amos was still nowhere in sight. That fat tramp started to run for the woods, and Dink caught him right about the middle of the shinbone with a rock the size of a plum.

That tramp could sure swear.

When they saw how badly they were outnumbered, the tramps kind of gave up and waited out in front of the porch.

Caleb started handing out rocks. He had a whole armload of them.

"What'd you do with the other kid that was in there?" Clint demanded, from about twenty-five feet out.

The one they had called Harry spit in the frosty grass.

"What other kid?" he said.

"You know what other kid," said Clint. It was just being able to say things like that, that had made him Holy President of our club.

"I never saw nobody else," said Harry.

"Well, you better find him fast, Mister, or you're gonna be wearing this rock," said Clint.

"You got a big mouth, don't you, kid?"

"Yeah, and I got about sixteen other big mouths right behind me. You find that other boy, or you're never gonna see another freight train again."

The tramps looked at each other, a little bit worried. Dink picked up a new rock, and the fat tramp backed off a step or two.

"Get me out of here!" said a voice from the darkness.

"That was Amos!" I said.

"Where are you?" yelled Myron.

"Down here, under the porch. I fell through and bent my ankle," said Amos.

As we came up to the house, the tramps faded quietly into the woods, and we never saw them around Harleyville again.

Amos's ankle wasn't hurt bad, and we all made it back to town without getting caught by parents or anybody.

The proud members of 693402 began to separate and sneak back to their own homes. Finally there were just us Birddogs and Caleb and Clint Harker left.

"We didn't get the nest," Dink admitted to Clint.

"And Caleb followed us," confessed Amos.

"So I guess we won't get to be Hounds, huh?" I asked Clint.

"Oh, I don't know," he said. "You conducted yourselves bravely; you found us some enemies. I think the Club will vote to let you be Hounds."

Dink and Amos and I looked at each other and smiled proudly.

"Besides," Clint went on. "It looks like we've got us a new Birddog." He looked at Caleb.

"Hot dog!" exclaimed Caleb.

Me and Dink and Amos looked at Caleb and smiled again.

9

It had gotten cold the week before Christmas. A big storm from Canada had moved down over the midwest and brought lots of snow and sleet and ice. For two days, big blankets of gray clouds moved over us from the north, and everybody said there'd be snow and plenty of it by Christmas.

Mama and Papa were going crazy hiding presents for us, and me and Caleb were going just as crazy locating them all. It was the Wednesday that school let out; Christmas was the following Monday. At the supper table, Callie was acting very nervous.

"I just . . . well, I thought maybe there was something I wanted to tell everyone," she said.

"You've always got something to say," Caleb commented.

"Not like this," she went on. "Because I need everyone's help."

"What is it?" asked Papa, finishing up his

cherry pie. I could tell, just by looking at Mama, that she knew what it was all about.

"I'm not positive, you understand," Callie said, "but I *think* I like Herbie Coggins. And he's asked me to the Christmas dance at school."

"Big deal," I said.

"Close your yap," said Papa. "I think that's just wonderful, dear."

"You see," said Callie, "he's coming to pick me up at seven-thirty this Saturday. And I've just got to have everything go all right." For some reason she was looking from me to Caleb when she said it. "You mustn't hurt him, or tease him, or roll his car away, or try to get him to wrestle."

"Why, of course not," said Caleb.

"I'll see that the boys behave," said Papa.

"And I want to have you wear your new suit, Papa," Callie said.

"What new suit?"

"You might as well go ahead and get that new flannel one we looked at downtown last week, Orville," said Mama. "You've been needing another one for a long time."

Papa looked from Mama to Callie, like he'd been tricked into something.

The next morning after breakfast I got the $5.25 out of my bank and decided to go ahead and get something for Caleb for Christmas.

Mama had told me I shouldn't give him an old dog bone or a mudball, like I did last year.

"I wish, for once," she said, "you'd try to get something that Caleb would really appreciate. I want you to buy it with your own money and not even tell Papa or me what it is. Then I'd know you were growing up and were old enough to feel the true Christmas spirit."

Outside, the air was so cold it cut into your chest when you breathed it. I stood on our front stoop and looked around at all the new snow just waiting to be horsed around in. Down Rainwater Street, on the vacant lot on the corner, I could see Amos Finch and Harvey Willis rolling big balls of snow to make a fort with. That snow was on the wet side, and just right for making forts.

When I got down to the corner, I stood and watched Amos and Harvey work for a while.

"What are you guys doing?" I asked.

"What does it look like we're doing?" said Amos, without even looking up at me.

"You guys going to make a fort?"

"Over there, between those two trees. You want to help?"

"Sure," I said.

And we spent the whole morning working on that fort. It was real neat, too, when we'd finished caulking up the seams between the big snowballs. We even took some of the "For Sale" signs from the lots around the corner and made a roof over part of our fort.

That afternoon we made snowballs. I don't mean we made a few snowballs. We made hundreds of them, and stored them inside the fort.

Dink joined us in the afternoon and sat on a box over at one end of our fort and turned out an amazing number of perfectly round snowballs, like he was a redheaded snowball machine.

Amos and I were making snowballs too, but they weren't nearly as good as Dink's. Harvey Willis was still improving on the fort.

"How many do you reckon we ought to make?" Amos inquired.

"We'll need a lot," said Dink.

"I don't mean to sound nosy," said Harvey, "but what for?"

"Just in case of a fight, we will," said Dink. "You can always use more than you make, if a fight turns up."

"Who are we gonna fight?" I asked him.

"Anybody who wants to," said Dink. "We're not scared of anybody!"

"No, sir, we're not!" added Harvey, the youngest of us.

But that afternoon we just made snowballs.

We didn't run across anybody who wanted a snowball fight. Finally Dink had to go home, and Harvey decided to go with him.

"We'll have us a battle tomorrow," yelled Dink as he was leaving, but he forgot to mention who with.

After they were gone, me and Amos quit making snowballs and walked around our fort, proud of how strong it was and how real it looked.

It was starting to get dark early, as it always does on those overcast winter days. The snow seemed to muffle the car noises from over on Main Street; you could hear a hound yapping at something in the woods at the edge of town. The smoke came up from all the chimneys along Rainwater Street and kind of floated straight up, where it finally melted into the same color as the sky, and you couldn't see it anymore.

"I better go home too," Amos sighed. "She's really a beaut, isn't she?" he said, looking at our fort again.

When he left, it was kind of spooky, standing there in the early darkness. The two big oak trees that made up the ends of the fort stretched blackly up into the sky, like roots, reaching clear up to heaven.

For the first time all day I felt cold. I shivered and put my hands in my pockets. My gloves had gotten soaked, and I had set them in the fort. By now they were frozen solid to the hard-packed ice of the floor. It was getting much colder.

Way up the street I could make out the figure of Slim, a fellow who did odd jobs around town, and he was headed right down Rainwater Street. He was leading something on a rope, but I couldn't tell what it was because of the darkness. I waited, and let him come on, and carefully gripped one of the snowballs from the top of Dink's pile.

Being cold and all, I guess, is why my throw went wide. I missed Slim entirely, but I hit that thing he was leading. I hit it right near the center of the rear section. The snowball made a kind of stinging "Smaaack!" as it hit, and disintegrated on the flank of whatever it was.

It didn't take to that snowball so well. Like a spring uncoiling, it suddenly lurched forward and caught Slim just below the small of the back, sending him straight through the air for about eight feet and landing him face down in a snowbank at the edge of the sidewalk.

Slim just lay where he had suddenly been sent. I was starting to get worried when the legs that were sticking out of the hole in the snow began to move and Slim crawled out and stood up, brushing off snow and speaking to that thing in a low voice.

At last I figured out what it was that he had been leading; it was the biggest blooming goat I had ever seen! Since Slim hadn't even seen my snowball, I decided to go out and have a closer look. Why, that goat must have stood four feet high at the shoulder.

"Hey, Slim!" I yelled. "What you got?"

"Who's that? Oh, Wallin's, ain't it?" he squinted at me in the darkness. "Your brother ain't roun' here, is he?" He looked around for Caleb, with worry written all over his face.

Caleb had thrown a play snake on Slim, one day when Slim was working on the bushes in front of our house. That's why Slim didn't trust Caleb.

"No, he's at home, Slim," I said. "Is that your goat?"

"Sometimes I don' know if he's mine or I'm his. Why, that there goat like to bust me open, and I'm just leadin' him down the street here." Slim carefully rubbed the place where it hurt. "Biggest and meanest goat I ever seen, that Carlyle."

"Hey, Slim, would you sell him to me? Carlyle? Would you sell your goat to me so I can give him to Caleb for a Christmas present?"

"Sell him? Why, I'd . . . how much you give for him?"

"I've got five dollars and twenty-five cents. I'll give you that for him." I could hear my heart beating as I stood there in the cold. What a present that goat would make for Caleb!

"You want to give this here goat to your brother?"

"Yeah. He'd like a pet for Christmas."

"Well, now." Slim smiled. "You gonna give him to that brother, I reckon I could let you have him." He kind of laughed. "That Caleb, he give me a pet one time too, you know." He chuckled.

I gave Slim the money, and he gave me the rope with Carlyle on the other end. And then he walked off down the street, chuckling to himself as he went.

It happened so quick, I didn't have time to stop and really think about it very carefully. It had just seemed like a good idea.

So there I stood, holding onto a rope that was tied to the biggest goat in Ogano County. I wondered what Papa would think of me buying Slim's goat. I decided not to take Carlyle home for a while.

"Here, Carlyle, come on, Carlyle!" I coaxed, pulling gently at the rope. Surprisingly enough, Carlyle did come, just the way I pulled him, which happened to be in the direction of our fort. There I tied him to one of the oak trees, where he would be hidden from the street.

Then I went home to supper.

10

I had a hard time getting out of the house the next morning. Callie had to remind us again to behave when her date came by, and Caleb was getting anxious for an invitation to share in the ownership of our fort. I didn't ask him; Caleb's too young for real tough stuff like that.

When I finally made it, I started running and slipping down the icy sidewalk toward our fort. Amos was already there. He saw me coming and ran out to meet me.

"Holy Catfish!" said Amos.

"What's the matter?" I asked him.

"You'll never believe it."

"Believe what?"

"There's a moose or something in our fort!"

"That's Carlyle," I said, and I told him about my deal with Slim.

"You should have told me about it earlier," said Amos. "I came over early and climbed into the fort right on top of that moose of yours."

"He's a goat."

"Well, anyway, he growled at me. I went right up that oak tree. And he stinks terrible!"

Soon Dink and Harvey arrived.

"Wait till we tell you!" said Dink.

"Wait till *we* tell *you!*" said Amos.

"Good night!" said Dink. "Who put that elk in our snow fort?"

"He's a goat!" I insisted. I explained again.

"Let me tell you my news," said Dink. "We're fighting that gang of kids from South Harleyville! Myron Webster and some of his friends. They agreed to attack us at two o'clock this afternoon. We got it all arranged on the phone last night. There's four of them, too."

"We better get busy, then," said Harvey.

We started in by reinforcing the entire fort with more snow. Dink went back to making more snowballs. Carlyle looked at us and shifted about impatiently at the end of his rope.

"I better feed my goat," I said.

"What're you going to feed him?" asked Amos.

"He smells like he ate a couple of skunks already," said Harvey.

"I don't know," I said. "Hey! Look what

happened to my gloves! I left them frozen to the floor last night, and now all that's left is the fingers and thumbs."

"That ought to answer your question," said Dink. "Go find him a bushel of gloves somewhere."

I went back home and swiped half a head of lettuce, some heels of bread, a bunch of orange peels, a few Christmas cookies, and some bird seed that Callie had for her parrot. Carlyle sniffed everything carefully and then ate it all but the orange peels.

We were all pretty excited when we met in the fort after lunch.

"Now, I'll cover the center section, because I'm the best shot," said Dink, who wasn't lying. That's why we let him be leader. "Amos, you cover anything on the left, since you're left-handed. Bud, you take the right side. Harvey, you stay down behind the fort and make sure to keep us all supplied with snowballs."

"Baloney!" said Harvey, but we all knew he would.

It was a bright afternoon, with the sun reflecting off the snow so hard it made you squint your eyes to see. I had tied Carlyle down inside our fort and stationed myself over on the right side as Dink had ordered.

"Here they come!" yelled Harvey.

"Get down there and take care of those snowballs!" Dink commanded. "And don't fire until I tell you to. We'll use yesterday's old hard snowballs for long range shooting, today's when they're closer, and hard ones again when they charge."

I didn't know how Dink knew they *would* charge, but he acted like he knew what he was doing. Over on my side, I didn't see anything to throw at. Coming down the street, off to the left, were two kids. One was Myron Webster, and I didn't remember the name of the other one.

"There's two more of them someplace," Dink cautioned.

Myron and his pal stopped just out of range. They knew how far Dink could throw. They whispered together for a few minutes, pointing in different directions now and then. Then the one whose name I didn't know went back up the street out of sight. In a few minutes he came back with a pushcart loaded with snowballs.

"My goodness!" moaned Amos. Just after he said it, something whistled by my ear like an angry hummingbird. It plopped into the snow about twenty-five feet behind me. While I'd watched the two decoys, those other two South Harleyville apes had crept up from our right side. They were behind some trees, right on the corner of our vacant lot.

"I see them," said Dink calmly. "Don't throw yet. They'll come closer."

And that's just what they did. From then on it was war, in its bloodiest form, as both parties of our enemey charged.

"Let 'em have it!" screamed Dink. As he said it, he let fly with one of his specialties that caught one of those kids in the neck and knocked his hat off. That's how hard it hit.

I began to throw like crazy. Sometimes I'd hit, but mostly I'd miss. The ones I did land, however, seemed to really jolt them guys. I was mighty glad we had Dink on our side to make those perfect snowballs.

Harvey was scurrying back and forth, bringing us new supplies from the three great heaps of snowballs we had made. Amos seemed to be holding his own on our left flank, while Dink and I peppered away at our two opponents on the right. They would jump out from behind a tree and throw and then jump back. We weren't hitting them, and they weren't hitting us.

"This ain't getting us nowhere," commented Dink. "We got to run them out from those trees. Let's go, Bud. Amos, you and Harvey stay and guard the fort."

Together we charged out of there like a

couple of lunatics, carrying as much ammunition as we could. I caught a snowball in the shoulder, but it didn't slow me down. That Dink could run at top speed and throw a snowball, sidearm, at the same time with such accuracy that nobody would dare to stand in his way.

Our enemy began to retreat, ducking from tree to tree until they reached the street and had to make a break for it.

"That ought to learn 'em," said Dink, letting fly with his last snowball. But when we turned to go back to the fort, we realized we'd been faked out.

While we had chased two kids from the trees, Myron and his pal had advanced on the fort, using the pushcart as both protection and supply dump. Amos and Harvey were no match for the blistering attack and were being forced from the fort.

"Good gosh, Bud, quick. We got to get back there and help, or we'll lose the fort," cried Dink. But we both knew it was too late.

As we ran, I noticed Amos was doing something inside the fort while Harvey tried to fight off the two attackers alone. Then I saw what he was doing.

Amos had untied Carlyle, the last minute before he and Harvey ducked out of the fort.

Carlyle must have been in a bad mood from

being tied up for so long. Or maybe he didn't like the diet I had fed him. Also, I think that somebody must have tried to teach Carlyle to pull a cart once and he was against the idea. Because when he came stalking out of our snow fort, he took one look at the advancing pushcart and knew just what to do.

Myron and his friend were crouched down behind it, so they didn't see Carlyle sniff the air and then paw at the ground for a second before he put his head down and charged.

When he hit that pushcart, it sounded like an automobile accident and looked like an explosion. Myron, his friend, Carlyle, and a hundred snowballs all shot out in different directions.

The concussion separated the pushcart body from its wheels, the wheels rolling off sickly in two different directions while the body just collapsed into so much kindling.

And that's how we destroyed the pushcart and won the battle. By the time Dink and I arrived, our opponents had retreated out of range. They were all out of ammunition and in a state of shock from Carlyle's efforts. Just before they left for good, Myron Webster waved a fist at us in final warning. But we had won! There was no doubt about it.

"We really took them!" shouted Dink, jumping around and slapping us all on the back.

"There's only one thing." He looked right at me. "I know they'll be back. And Bud, that goat of yours did a fine job, but he takes up so much room and smells so bad it's a wonder we didn't have to surrender before they even got here."

I looked to Amos and Harvey for support, but they just nodded in agreement with Dink, and held their noses.

"Okay," I said. "Just let me tie him out in the lot until tomorrow night. Give me until then to find a new place for him. And remember not to tell Caleb about him."

"We don't have to tell him about that goat. Everybody in the county can smell him," said Dink.

The next day was the day before Christmas Eve, and everything around our house was busy. Dink and Amos and Harvey held the fort, so to speak, while I tried to find a new place to hide Carlyle. Every so often I'd run down to the corner to make sure we weren't being attacked.

I couldn't find anywhere to put that old goat. There was absolutely no place to hide him in the garage. That left the house. I wandered through the rooms from top to bottom, trying to spot a place to hide a goat.

After lunch Mama noticed me looking around.

"Now you get out of here, Bud! You've been snooping around all day. You keep it up and there won't be anything for you on Christmas."

"I'm not looking for any presents," I said, kind of mad at being falsely accused. Heck, I knew where every present I was going to get was, and what it was!

"Well, go outside anyway. Make a snowman or something," Mama said. "Callie and I are going downtown to do some last-minute shopping."

That's all I needed to know. Caleb was upstairs reading a book, and Papa had gone down to the office. With nobody around, I could investigate a lot more carefully.

After they'd gone, I went through the house again. That's when I decided on the hall closet.

Our hall closet is built kind of underneath the stairs, and it's a big one. In the far end, away from the door, where the closet tapers down to nothing, Mama used to store luggage. But she had gotten Papa to haul it all up to the attic one Saturday afternoon. In that little end, there was room for Carlyle, even if I did have to stuff him in. And I hid him by piling up the remaining boxes into a wall across the closet.

Carlyle offered no resistance as I led him into his new home.

Just as I closed the door, Petunia wandered in from a nap in the living room. She took about two steps down the hall and then froze, sniffing at the air. And then she began to growl and stiffen her legs. The hair along her spine stood straight up.

"Hey! Cut it out!" I whispered, afraid that she would give the whole thing away. Paying no attention to me, she continued to point toward the closet.

Just then the back door slammed closed, and I heard Papa's footsteps in the kitchen.

I threw myself on all fours and, growling, advanced toward Petunia.

"Rufff! Rurrrrrr," I said, as Papa walked by me. Petunia continued to ignore me and to growl and look at the closet.

"What are you doing, Bud?" Papa inquired.

"Oh, we're just playing, Papa. Rufff. Rufff-rufff! Petunia and I play dogfight all the time."

"You do?" asked Papa.

"Oh, sure, Rurrr, rufff! We like it. See how Petunia likes to play dogfight, Papa?"

"Yes, I noticed that. Really looks like she's upset, doesn't she?"

"Yes, sir," I answered, and Papa went on upstairs.

That settled it. I had to get Petunia out of there.

"Here, girl," I whispered. She wouldn't even

look at me. Her nose told her there was an intruder inside that closet, and she had made up her mind to wait for him to come out.

It took a short length of clothesline rope from the kitchen, and a great deal of determination, to pull Petunia out of the house.

Fifteen minutes later I was back on the corner with Dink and the gang. We still hadn't been attacked.

"I don't know what's the matter with them guys," complained Amos.

"They're not beaten yet," said Dink. "They just want to catch us when we're not ready." This must have been true, because they still hadn't come after us by suppertime, so we all went home, uneasy and disappointed.

Callie met me at the door.

"You'll be on your best behavior tonight, won't you, Bud?"

"Huh?" I said. Callie frisked me and made me show her everything in my pockets.

"You promised you'd be good. Remember now?"

"Oh, yeah," I said. "Don't worry so much." She followed me down the hall.

"Bud?" she asked.

"What?"

"Bud, are you making that smell?"

"Huh?" I said.

"I asked you if you were making that terrible odor? Can't you smell it?" I sniffed. The whole hallway was full of something that hung in the air. I recognized it. It was Carlyle. I hadn't noticed it when he was outside in the fresh air. At least I tried not to. But inside, I could notice the smell just fine.

"Naw, I don't smell anything," I lied. "M'dose is kind of sdobbed ub!"

"Well, I smell it, and it's awful," said Callie. She went back upstairs to put some more gunk on her face.

Papa came in and hung his coat in the hall closet. He put the big box with his new suit in it on the floor and turned around and looked at me for a minute.

"Go take a bath, Bud," he said, and walked by me into the living room.

Caleb came downstairs, yawning. He stopped on the last step and sniffed.

"Good grief, Bud!" he said. Just then Mama came in from the kitchen to tell us supper was ready.

"Supper's ready," said Mama. She looked at me; then she looked at Caleb; then she looked back at me. "Go wash your hands, boys," she said.

The main subject at supper, of course, was that smell.

"A rat must have crawled into the wall and died," said Papa.

"Maybe it was a whole herd of rats," said Caleb.

Callie was already dressed up, so she wouldn't have to keep good old Herbie Coggins waiting, in case he arrived early.

Just before dessert, I thought I heard a noise from the hall closet.

"What was that?" asked Papa.

"What was what?" I said.

"That noise. Out in the hall."

"Maybe it was snow falling off the house," I offered.

"No, it was kind of an unhhhHHH! sound," said Papa.

"You didn't put on your new suit!" Callie noticed, suddenly.

"I'll have time after supper," said Papa.

"No, you won't! It's almost seven-thirty now. Won't you go put it on now? Please?"

"Oh, all right," Papa answered, looking sadly at the custard Mama was just bringing in.

I heard his footsteps go across the hall. I heard the closet door open. Then I heard the light in the closet click on. Then I didn't hear anything except Caleb eating his custard.

Papa came back to the supper table. He looked sort of dazed. Under his arm was the box with his new suit inside it.

"Orville?" said Mama. "What's wrong?"

Papa looked from Caleb to me and back again. He had a funny look on his face. Then he put his hand up to his head and sort of groaned. I breathed easier. I knew how he was going to take Carlyle now.

"Did you ever see a cow with a beard?" Papa asked Mama, putting on his simple-minded look. "Even in this house?"

"It's finally happened," Mama said quietly, kind of to herself. "He's lost his mind. Quick, children, up to your rooms! I don't want you to see him like this!"

Callie held her forehead. Mama and Papa can carry on this act a long time when they want to rub it in that we are driving them to the boobyhatch, and suppose Herbie caught some of it?

"I saw one in the hall closet," said Papa proudly. "It wanted to eat my new suit, but I wouldn't let it. I told it to go away."

"Go, children, go quickly!" begged Mama.

Somebody began to pound on our front door.

"That's Herbie!" moaned Callie, rushing to let him in.

"Why did that bearded cow want to eat my new suit?" Papa asked Mama.

"It's all right. It's all right, dear," said Mama. "I'll see you through this thing if it means nursing you for the rest of my life!"

"We haven't always had that bearded cow in the hall closet, have we?" asked Papa.

Callie came in dragging somebody who looked like he was in a clown suit, there were so many snowball marks on him.

"Some of those nasty boys from South Harleyville tried to kill Herbie, when he got out of his car!" wailed Callie, all excited. "Why they almost snowballed him to death, and Herbie didn't do a thing to them!"

"Goodness gracious!" muttered Caleb. I could tell he didn't think much of this Herbie.

"And there was this huge dog, dragging a doghouse all over the place," Herbie added.

Just then Carlyle wandered in from the hall and came over to me. Herbie Coggins jumped up on the table.

"Looka the elk!" he shouted.

"That's the one," said Papa, smiling.

"Merry Christmas, Caleb," I said weakly, keeping my eyes on my custard.

"Make him promise he won't try to eat my suit again," Papa asked Mama.

"HnhhhHHH!" said Carlyle.

Mama just stared at all of us, like she couldn't believe it.